Last Fake Happy World

By T.B.O.A. SAD

Last Fake Happy World
Copyright © 2018 Richard A. Schroeder Jr

All rights reserved.
No part of this book may be reproduced in any form without documented permission from the author. Richard Schroeder is T.B.O.A. Sad.

This is a work of fiction. All characters, situations and contents are creations of Richard Schroeder. Any resemblance to actual events or humans is purely coincidental.

ISBN 978-0-692-12430-7

Printed in the United States by:
Morris Publishing®
3212 East Highway 30
Kearney, NE 68847
1-800-650-7888

Visit tboasad.com to experience the monstrous world of T.B.O.A. Sad!

Table of Contents

When Summer Falls	1
Perpetual Adoration	11
Garbage Strike!	21
Black Baby	31
Strange Birds	51
Post Traumatic Halloween Disorder	65
The Standoff Opera	83
Familiar Faces	99
The Curse of Hexcera	111
Yessica Doll	121
Follow Me Down	135
Dangerous Distractions	147
Away From It All	155

Don't Look Now	**165**
Occult Pride	**173**
Relive and Revenge	**183**
To Hell With Vacation	**193**

When Summer Falls

Summer was the girl that boys would dream of. Beautiful tan skin, native-black hair and deep-hazel eyes. She was independent and outgoing, confident yet shy, constantly contradicting herself and so incessantly inconsistent.

And here she was, the same as always, leaning against the window and watching another day dawn.

"Up all night again?" her mother called from the kitchen, the breakfast smells slowly filtering into the living room.

"I slept a little," she replied. "I was watching movies. Sewing my jeans back together."

A brief clanging of pans and silverware from the dishwasher gave way to the typical response. "You need to sleep more. You're not going to be young forever, you know."

The summer was winding down so quickly for Summer, who hated her name at least a little, and though still young she couldn't help but obsess over the irreversible flow of time. It was almost as if she found herself looking back at today from an old age, remembering youth and yesterday as a dull memory in the future. And maybe there was truth to that in some strange way, because no matter how hard she tried, she could never completely enjoy a present moment. The instant she thought of it, the instant was over, and time continued to rage on with or without her approval.

By afternoon, Summer rose from a couch nap, rays of warm sunshine beaming through the windows of the living room. She sat on the stiff cushions, stretching her stiff neck and forcing herself to self-motivate.

It was still early enough that she could do anything she wanted. Another limitless day, her parents gone doing who knew what and whatever. And without hesitance, she knew that there was only one

LAST FAKE HAPPY WORLD

place in the entire surrounding world that she wanted to be. A secret place where time somehow could stand still, to a degree, and there would be no talking, no complaining, no arguments, and best of all, absolutely no people. Or at least no living people.

~ The primitive New Hillock Cemetery ~

   Beneath the afternoon sun, Summer was already on her way, leaving behind the dusty confines of the house and its relentless distractions. The sun felt good on her skin, warming her legs in her short blue jean cut-offs, the same for her arms in a black skull and crossbones tank top. The days were winding down before she would have to cover up in layers for the ever-looming fall and winter. But for now, for today, she was alive in this summertime and so full of joy for the day ahead.

   It had been some time since her family moved here. A stranded house, isolated and cut off from civilization. In truth, the driveway led straight to a highway that led straight to a town, that in turn led straight to everything she wished to escape. But back here, beyond the tree-lining of her family's backyard, here was her secret world.
   How long had it truthfully been? Time again distorted. As she walked into the world of trees she remembered the first day, her father promising to take her exploring once they had unpacked. They had walked and wandered the forest back, following no particular path on that snowy day. Young and uneasy, she would look back to make sure their footprints were still there in the snow, so afraid to be astray even within the comforting shadow of her father.
   And then they had discovered it - The lost to time 'New Hillock Cemetery.' Not beyond the trees but within them, a cemetery from a century ago. There were suddenly steep hills and knolls, unusual trees and roots large enough to trip you beneath the snowfall.

LAST FAKE HAPPY WORLD

There was a decaying bridge from a lost trail or old visitor road and beneath it, winding like a snake, was a creek far too clean to be a creek, too small to be a river and too large to be a stream.

That had been the first time, that abbreviated discovery, but from then on it had become Summer's perfect place. It wasn't always easy to find, and she sometimes got turned around, trying to remember those snowy footprints like breadcrumbs in the woods. But by now, these few years later, it was more than second nature. It was a beacon and a pull, a secret pathway by heart that she imagined she could find even if her eyes were blind.

And here she was, yet again. The unfenced-in cemetery, its welcoming archway reading "New Hillock Cemetery" in faded and falling letters.

The familiar sounds came first. The slow rush of water over rock, the song of unseen birds through treetops. A smile spread across her lips. This feeling... This was the reason why she came here.

And here the world changed. The high hills were unnatural, like thick fingers on the land. The air was filled with tiny bugs and drifting pollen, light highlighting them from time to time, giving the area a fairytale aura.

And the graves. The forgotten names of people from a long time ago. Graves that were chipped sculptures, headstones that were crude rock. There were hardly-there markers that could have been tombstones some time ago, and others that were variations on crosses and religious fashion. Summer knew the names of some of the departed by heart, though most of the engraving was lost to weather and time.

She walked through this place with no specific aim, content as she passed the familiar markers, up and down the steep hills. Who would build a cemetery so close to a creek, she used to wonder. Her father suggested on that first visit that maybe the creek was magic, that it washed away and carried off all of the pain from the

LAST FAKE HAPPY WORLD

people who were buried here.

She was older now and sometimes still wondered, though then stopping herself every time she realized she was doing it again.

Regardless of why, everyone's problems here were far away now. The creek flowed today just as it must have way back then, the same way it would long after she was gone as well.

By midday, Summer had cleared her mind as she traversed the forgotten memorials. The strange and twisted trees that were alive though leafless, the thirsty roots that rose from the ground and descended to the creek. She followed those roots down to the bank, the shallow clear water always warm to the touch.

Careful on the slippery rocks, she kicked off her sandal shoes and wandered beneath the crumbled bridge. Here she was again, no plan, but always the same result. Through the forest, through the cemetery archway, through the graves and down to beneath the bridge.

Right here, time seemed to stop, but she knew now even this day was passing. Right this moment, already gone. This next moment, gone as well. Today, tomorrow and so on until she was no different than these resting people. Buried below and forgotten.

"What's wrong with me?" Summer said out loud to herself, caught off guard at her own randomness. "And now I'm talking to myself."

Her words gave a small echo in the shade of the bridge, sunlight coming down in lines through dotted holes.

"I don't think I'll get to come here forever, but it's all I want to do," she continued. "I'm already getting older now. I feel like there's still a kid inside of me that wants to do nothing but cry. But I don't want to keep crying."

She tried to anyway, just to let it out, but it unsurprisingly didn't happen.

"I don't know what I want to do. I don't want to work at a job. I

LAST FAKE HAPPY WORLD

don't want to get old. I don't want to fall in love..."
Summer's mind raced with self-justification. Ideas of how screwed up living was by human design. How basic principles of life were so mangled and distorted, the true definition of survival completely repurposed to be something artificial and unnatural.

How could anyone stand by what people had turned this world into?

"In my books, in my movies this is the part where the stranger shows up and we talk, and we run away together, we run away from everything and this summer never ends."

She paused and listened, the sound of water and silence.

"I don't care. Nothing matters."

She stopped talking and was lost in thought again, thinking about this season's passage and watching the water flow past. Her foot kicked in the shallow depths, splashing the warmth across her leg as she stood, then stepping with both feet into the clear creek.

It felt so comforting, Summer slowly wading her feet through the ankle-deep shallows, stepping out from beneath the bridge and taking it all in. The song of a distant bird, the breeze through the twisted trees, the roots in the water and the silence of the stones. She didn't need a stranger to find her, this was good enough.

"I don't want this to ever end."

Time tried to oblige as the afternoon peacefully dragged on. Her brain went through the familiar motions. Build up frustration, calm down again. Ideas brewing like an internal storm, then relaxation. She kicked around in the water, picking up rocks and eventually heading back onto dry land again.

"Eventually, they'll see that I don't even care," she said aloud in her nonexistent conversation, her path leading back up a cemetery hill. "I'll be indifferent. Indifference will be my favorite word."

LAST FAKE HAPPY WORLD

Summer climbed the steep incline over the rooted ground, pulling herself up with the aid of a tree's leafless branch. This was such a beautiful view here, the raised ground leading to the old bridge, overlooking half of the cemetery on each side.

She smiled to herself, carelessly walking onto its questionable stability. It felt so safe, like walking the dark stairs in her house, or climbing the ancient trees in her yard. Her naked feet pressed against the chipped rock and century old structure. This would be a place her mother would say – 'Get down from there! You'll kill yourself!'

But she had no concern. "If I had a daughter," she imagined silently, "I would tell her to climb up here with me, stand here and scream at the world…"

Summer walked to the edge and looked down, it wasn't so far. Twenty, maybe thirty feet? She could see her sandals still just sitting there, set beside the creek that had felt so pure and warm. Even now, from this height, she could see insects dancing across the surface, tiny fish or crayfish moving beneath. It was all spread out before her, the beauty of this secret cemetery.

Summer closed her eyes and breathed, reaching her arms out and stretching her back.

~ Suddenly, the ground gave out beneath her ~

The weatherworn bridge crumbled where she stood, Summer's eyes opening and her arms flailing as she tumbled forward and then back.

The cemetery world spun in her eyes, around and then upside down, her head cracking backwards hard against the old bridge. In that single second, every emotion collided. Shock, surprise, danger and pain intertwined as she yelled out. It was a strange sound but not a scream, the sound of life in the inescapable jaws of death.

LAST FAKE HAPPY WORLD

~ And then the splash ~

Her body landed unnaturally, no impact absorbed by the shallow water. Summer was on her back, her eyes open and staring back up at the deadly bridge. The small spot that had collapsed was like an upside-down smile, a mocking downward grin as she lay there motionless those initial moments.

In absolute shock, she almost laughed.

What just happened? She could've died, this was so crazy... And she stayed still, the water only deep enough to reach her ears. Her mouth, her nose and her eyes were all above the creek level. It felt almost peaceful, the submerged silence as the warm water poured over her.

And then the peaceful look in her eyes passed. Hands, arms, legs, neck – Summer couldn't move. The look in her eyes stressed panic now, hopelessness. No, how could this be? She tried to force her body to move again, anything. Any muscle. A finger? No, no, no... This couldn't be happening. She could only blink and breathe and nothing else, her mind unable to process this thought.

Who was going to find her? Who would look? Her parents would try, but how long until then? Even if they found her, what could they do? A thousand thoughts were born in her mind in a moment. Panic and death, paralysis and absolute terror overtook her.

It was a dark night. Summer had cycled through every emotion and fear she had ever known, two times and then again.

"No..." she tried to say, only a whisper emerging from her hardly open lips.

Through the holes of the bridge and the trees high above it, she could see the stars out here at night. With no mobility, she tried to calm herself mentally with only small results. Someone would find her, her parents would be calling their friends by now. She began to wonder if her father even remembered this place.

LAST FAKE HAPPY WORLD

The morning came, and the sleepless girl lay broken in the cemetery creek. The night had brought a visitor, maybe a fox or a dog, walking into the water and smelling her before moving on. Small fish and other unseen water life began to give small pecks that would have made her laugh one day ago. But not now, she wouldn't laugh anymore even if she could. Her stomach growled from its empty hole, her brain aching hard from the impact and submersion.
"How long until they come…" she wondered in dreadful silence.

A second day passed.

The pecking became stronger, and it rained a slight drizzle. Dragonflies and humidity followed, the water level almost rising to her lips. That panic of death was so powerful now, she demanded herself to mediate, to forcefully relax. Her brain and stomach argued, the pain and aches increasing.
The locked angle of her body sometimes shifted with the flow of water, but only in the slightest. She tried to take comfort, if this was it. If this was her end, and there was nothing she could do to fight it, she had to embrace it. Somehow.

Another night, the stars out above and she could only stare back at them. Life, in the end, was meaningless now.
In a cruel false hope, Summer thought she felt her left arm move this night –
But it was only the returning fox or dog, biting and lifting it in curiosity before dropping it back into the water and running away.

By the fourth or maybe fifth day, Summer was changed. She was at peace with herself, but more importantly, with her place in this world. She was at peace with life, peace with death, and at peace with her rest in the comforting waters of the cemetery creek.

LAST FAKE HAPPY WORLD

Fish and other things came and went, swimming against her body and squirming through her shirt and shorts. Her water-logged skin felt nothing, and it drizzled rain again. This time a small bit to cover maybe half an inch more of her face.

Fish fought the weak current to get near her head. She felt only a small, pecking pop when they pulled at her open eyes, violent for such small fish. Individually one eye was tugged at and plucked out, and then soon the other.

Summer was alive, deaf and blind beneath shallow water, slowly breathing through her nose. What came and went, she never knew. Leeches latching, turtles snapping, crayfish and water bugs tangled in her waving, seaweed-like long hair. At night, the small jaws of a nocturnal animal pulled at the stiff, wet meat of her once beautiful body.

And somehow still she lived, though less and less to nothingness. In the shallow water she lay in her creek bed, nurturing the life that inhabited this resting place of the dead.

Tiny pieces of the girl were carried away by animals, skin pulling off in time, clothes and bone blending in with the sediment.

The months passed, from the falling cemetery leaves of October to the frozen creek and snowfalls of December. In the months of spring the life came back, the forgotten bridge looming over the beautiful clear water creek. Animals arrived and passed, no human ever coming to this secret place to look.

Soon it was June, July again and then already August.

By September, Summer had washed away forever.

LAST FAKE HAPPY WORLD

Perpetual Adoration

The alarm sounds.
Blindly reach and turn it off.
That wet touch?
That strange smell...

Parson opened his exhausted eyes and his heart then stopped abruptly. He shouldn't have been panicked, but it was all so much to re-remember.
The blood, the body, the body's parts...
Set aside in various amounts were the severed parts of a person, transparent tarps covering the furniture and floor. Blood was collected and thickened anywhere it had sprayed or fallen, and the air condition was set to nearly refrigerate the entire house.
"Christ..." Parson moaned, sitting bedside with his head held in his hands. Nothing here was a surprise, but it was new again this morning.
Everything was ok. He had simply slept a few hours, no regrets. He needed his rest after all that work.
Parson stood in poor posture with his lanky body, no shirt and still dressed in tight black jeans from the night before.
It was too early. He walked past the remains without looking as best he could, straight to the bathroom and pointlessly closing the door behind. He looked to the mirror and the blotches of dry blood, nearly black across his white arms.
The day had just begun, but there was no time for a shower. Time would fly starting now and everything had to go just right.
The door – Oh God, the door!
Parson swung the bathroom door open and quickly ran through the house. Through the living room, the kitchen and then to the backdoor – Locked. That was a relief. He checked the front door, it

LAST FAKE HAPPY WORLD

was locked as always, checking all the shades, curtains and blinds. Everything was closed. The world was shut off, as it needed to be. He brushed his hand through his straight black hair, shaved around the sides and back. Today he would need all his wits about him.

By half an hour later, he had collected himself and collected the tools he would need for the next phase. Now donning a black vinyl apron and rubber gloves, he had forced himself to suppress the gagging and nausea, struggling to be strong under this act.
Fans on for smell and the air-condition still blasting, a poor attempt at preservation.
Parson sat at the clear tarped floor of the bedroom, ready to be crafty. Body parts were spread out evenly around him. Arms, hands, feet and so on. It was a female, the beautiful head with its full, wavy brown hair facing him, resting with a stump neck on the floor.
"Stay calm, you still have plenty of time," he comforted himself. "What we need is perfection. Precision."
And during the next set of hours, the determined artist went to work, assembling the naked body parts of the female shape like a jigsaw puzzle. It wasn't difficult to know what went where, but there were delicate angles where things should attach. Small pieces that held together larger things. The human body was such an alien construction, an organic grandfather clock, and he needed to get this just right.

KNOCK KNOCK

"No!!" Parson yelled out and quickly cupped his mouth. Who was here? He sat still at the floor, the naked woman half assembled before him.
Another knock, a visitor at the front door.
His heart raced. Was it the neighbors? The police??
His car was in the driveway, what day was it – Sunday? No, only

LAST FAKE HAPPY WORLD

Saturday... It could be the mailman...
"Mrs. Kellar?" a voice from outside called.
It was a strong male voice, unfamiliar. Parson remained in the silence, not moving and without a plan.
Another knock and then nothing, the waiting game and Parson could tell that the uninvited visitor lingered for a short moment. Thirty accelerated heartbeats later, and the sound of soft footsteps trailed away, the panic calming down.

At last he was alone with his puzzle again.

After some time, the body was set together as best he could remember. He looked it over, the chopped pieces set back where they were supposed to be, arms on the correct sides, legs as well.
He couldn't quite put his finger on it, but something was just a bit off...
Parson got up from his work and went to the living room, searching his bookcase and then retrieving a folded paper. It was a printed photo of the body before him, beautiful though alive, naked and smiling in the same nothing-pose she lay in now. He smiled back when he saw her there, such a beautiful girl he almost cried.
Ah, there it was. Her mouth was wrong, the skin and lips had been set upside down. Caked with the dried blood he had missed it, but it was so obvious now. He flipped them around on her lifeless head. Outstanding. Picture perfect.

In the bathroom once more, Parson zoned out looking at himself in the mirror, visualizing the next phase. He ran the blood off from the rubber gloves with hot bath water, wondering if doubt would enter his mind. Timewise, he was ahead of schedule but needed to stay focused. This next stage would prove impossible if he emotionally attached himself. Complete concentration was needed.

The tools were laid out before him. Sewing needles, scissors, a

LAST FAKE HAPPY WORLD

stitching hook and stitching thread, small clamps, gauze pads and more.
   Meticulously he went to work, day into the first hint of night. He didn't stop to rest, nor stop to eat or drink. Anything to break his inspiration would be too big of a gamble. The instant he thought too much about what it was he was doing, everything would have been for nothing.
   Mind off, compassionless. He sewed like a machine, just enough to hold her together. Rapid stabs through the clamped together skin, the stitching hook in and out. Left foot, left leg and to the torso. Right foot, right leg and to the torso to match. It was a fever of work, pushing the insides back in from the outside, holding them in and sealing it shut. He had to keep this up, her limp body growing stiff in death as the day went by.
   Parson's hands trembled a bit, his eyes beginning to look ahead, wanting to admire his work. But not yet. In time, this would all be worth it. Patience until that finish line.

Once her neck was set and her head was straight, once her lips were centered and sewn back onto her face, Parson leaned back and sighed a breath of exhaustion. She was nearly complete; a rapid-fire reconnection and his black vinyl apron was drenched in the blood. He honestly hadn't been sure he could do what had just been done. To see such things that shouldn't be seen, the inside of a girl. It was horrific, yet she was still so beautiful, on the inside as well as out.

Now she was completely together, only a long incision down her chest left open, letting that final step wait. It was all a process, everything in due time tonight.

Parson was on the back porch, no lights on and no neighbors around as he habitually took drags of a cigarette. It was time to wake up, time to psych himself up for the rest of this operation. He hurried, still nervous of any human contact during the night. One last breath of the cigarette and he looked to the full moon hidden behind the clouds. Tonight would be the night that everything he had come to know about the world would forever change. The night that his comprehension of life and all of its darkness would be enlightened in ways he had never imagined. But first, the needed things.

Black candles were lit. Black paint covered the living room's bloodless tarp in occult symbols and sacrilegious sigils. Parson had books open that the world had thought it burned, turned to pages of spells and rituals, illustrations of things a human mind couldn't possibly have conjured.

He would bring her body from the bedroom into here, but first he needed that one final ingredient, and it was time for the action he had been dreading the most.

The light came on in the cement basement, the switch flipped atop the stairs as he entered. Each footstep down matched his pounding heartbeat. He was well past the point of no return by now, but this would be even 'beyond the beyond.' Down the stairs, to the cold floor.

A muffled sound came from across this room beneath the house. He stood motionless in his hesitance, then swallowing hard and walking loudly towards it. No second guessing. This would be it now.

And there, bound and gagged with duct tape in a dog cage she sat. A perfect, nameless college girl, in her university cheerleading outfit. By charming ways he had met her, courted her and lured her in, all privately and hopefully without notice.

Tears ran down her cheeks to her gagged mouth as Parson grabbed at her arm, her blonde ponytail swinging like a pendulum. Covered screams went unheard as she contorted and pulled to fight back, led forward from her cage and across the basement floor.

LAST FAKE HAPPY WORLD

Parson remained stoic. She was not a girl to him, she was a vessel and livestock for his plan and purpose. She pushed, pulling and falling, kicking and trying anything to get away from the man in the apron, but it was fruitless. The drag through the basement, the climb up the stairs, the escorting into the living room draped in occult decorations.

The cheerleader bawled beneath her gag as Parson held her down here, more duct tape to bind her ankles together now that she was uncaged. She sat un-obediently at the floor, not taking her crying eyes away from the kidnapping man.

Parson left the room for a brief minute, leaving the hyperactive girl unattended. She could hardly move at all in her state, though her body bounded up and down, desperate for release.

When he reentered the symbol-covered living room, he was not alone. The cheerleader's eyes opened wide in a multiplied terror, seeing the stitched-together puzzle girl in his arms, carried almost romantically into the center of the room.

He set the lifeless form down, center of a double cross and black painted pentagram. Her arms and legs were spread to point with the ways of the symbol, the candles now set along her sides and head.

Words were chanted that sounded like unholy sounds, followed by sounds made that rung out like unholy words. Incantations and hands swimming through the air, the cheerleader watched on in helplessness, the black candle reflections burning in her eyes.

Parson turned his attention to her. He stood up from the reassembled girl and approached her, fear quivering through her soul. He touched her restrained body, not in a sexual way but in a way to know her flesh. Desperate, she tried to make eye contact, to communicate on any primal level with the psychopath to somehow save herself.

His left hand went to her university top, pulling it up to expose her pink bra and youthful frame. And just when she felt the trifling

LAST FAKE HAPPY WORLD

chance that his psychosexual desires could be her window to escape, his right hand stabbed upward between her breasts. Her flesh ripped open, the bra tearing at its center and a fountain of blood bubbling out. Her blocked screams were like a beast, the beautiful college girl making a final, deep painkiller moan as the last bits of breath raced in and out of her lungs.

Parson performed the impossible ritual, the young and bloody heart cut clean from the vessel, held in his shaking hands with his eyes bloodshot in gore. Far past science and dwelling now in the realm of black arts, he recited those words from his diabolical books, the life muscle in his rubber-gloved vice grip.

It was set down into the open inside-chest of his puzzle girl. There was nothing more to connect, nothing more to hook-stitch together. The large pieces were reunited, the countless small pieces reconnected, and the final piece was put in place. Everything from here on out, within this house beneath the full moon sky, would be ritually strict, word for word, and without a single error…

"When I kiss your lips, breathe my breath."

Nothing.

"When I touch your hand, touch my hand."

There was movement.

Violent vomit, her hair held back and a headache that pounded through her skull. Unnatural fluids poured from her mouth like ectoplasm, vaporizing and evaporating into otherworldly smoke with every heave.
"It's ok! I'm here! I'm here!"
"……Parson…" she said and remembered in a sick voice. "Did

LAST FAKE HAPPY WORLD

it... did it work..."
He burst with joy and tears. "It worked! Kacy, the books worked! You're back!! It worked!!"
She laughed a small and inaudible laugh. "You bastard... You Dr. Frankenstein bastard... I love you..."

Hours later and into the morning, Parson Kellar sat with his wife Kacy at the kitchen table, chair next to chair, feeding her small spoons of apple sauce. Her stitches were transformed into faint occult scars, her flesh cleaned up by washcloth. In segmented recollections, she recounted her black journey into the mysterious afterlife, her visions of Heaven and Hell and the infinite abyss. Parson jotted down fast notes to keep up with her, recording every single forbidden truth she had experienced in the beyond.

"That's enough for now," he comforted the love of his life, helping her from the table. "You need to sleep. I have to clean up this place and then I'll come to bed too."
They walked together slowly, Parson carefully aiding his now resurrected wife. Kacy gave a disgusted look as they passed the dead college girl.
"Gross... I really don't want to look at her..."
"Don't worry," he calmed. "Once we get you to sleep, I'll bury her in the backyard. This was the healthiest looking one I could catch."
"Looked kind of... cute, too. You didn't try to make out with her, did you?"
"Are you crazy??" Parson laughed. "Why make out with a cheerleader when I've got a wife who's been to hell and back? Literally?"
He kissed Kacy on the forehead and helped her into bed, tucking her in and sharing an embrace.
"I have so many more questions for you when you wake up," he

LAST FAKE HAPPY WORLD

told her. "And then we need to catch a boy, right? I'm dying to go next!"

LAST FAKE HAPPY WORLD

Garbage Strike!

"Mom, do you think the Garbage Man will come, even if no one puts out any garbage?"

Evan's mother sat at the edge of his bed. "So many questions," she answered. "Sometimes you think too much. Of course he'll come, silly. Everyone will put out garbage for him."

"And Friday will come too? Will I see her?"

Evan's mom walked to the child's door, turning off his bedroom light and giving him a loving look. "Friday will come too. But will you see her? We never know if we'll see either of them. But maybe, if we believe, maybe we'll be lucky enough to see them this year. Get some sleep, honey. It's getting late."

Evan turned over in bed, so excited for his favorite holiday. In no time at all he fell asleep, visions of garbage piling up in his head.

Garbage Day morning in the suburban town came, families waking up for a day of tradition and memories of holidays past. By as early as 8am, up and down the street residents could be seen hauling trash down their driveways. To the curb and setting it street-side, blue receptacles and items of all description.

"Hey, neighbor!" a man dragging two full bags of complete trash yelled across to the driveway next door. "Ready for the big day?"

"You better believe it! The wife's throwing out our couch this year! Should be a real sight!"

"The couch..." the other neighbor repeated. "Maybe we should throw our couch out too... No matter how much we hold onto, there's just never enough to throw out."

And this was the theme across the land, families competing to see who could outdo the other, throwing out everything from refrigerators to televisions, stacks of garbage bags and piles of old electronics. It was a cleansing tradition to get clean by staying dirty for a while, and now the time had come for the most joyous day of the year.

"Looking good, neighbor! You look as clean as a whistle!"
"Nice try – I haven't bathed all week and you know it!"
Friendly exchanges as the morning went on, the hours flying fast as the trash piled up. Decorations of festive pigs, rats, warthogs and cockroaches were set up in the yards, traditional green and brown holiday lights to be lit at night for the Garbage Man to see. But before the doors could be locked and the windows boarded up, the suburban families were soon loading into their cars and trucks and driving into town, picking up greasy bags of junky food, ready for the long night ahead.

"Welcome to Cramp Burger, may I take your order?"
A family ordered and drove up, pulling to the drive-thru window and getting their assorted Cramp Burgers and fries.
"Ugh, we're so sorry you have to work today," the driver made conversation with the boy at the window. "You should be closing early though, right?"
"Nah, they have us open 24 hours," the fast-food worker replied. "I hear some kids even had a full day of school today."
"What is this world coming to?" the driver sighed. "Well, don't work too hard tonight."
"Oh, don't worry about that! You guys have a happy Garbage Day!"
"Happy Garbage Day!" the kids yelled in unison from the backseat.

By 2pm, doors around town began to lock little by little. Boards were placed over the windows with care, mostly for tradition more than any practical reason.
"Dad!" a small child cried. "Leave enough space so I can watch! Maybe I'll see him!"

LAST FAKE HAPPY WORLD

The father looked at his son, remembering his own excitement once upon a time.
"Of course, but not too much. I don't want you to get scared."
"He just wants to see Friday," the sister teased. "I think he likes her!"
"Do not! I only like the Garbage Man!"

All around, in nearly every house, the same excited and curious conversations were had.

"I heard that he lives in the ground. He only comes out to beat up kids that are clean."

"I heard that Friday isn't really his daughter. She was the worst kid in the world, so he kept her!"

"Mom, how does the Garbage Man take away all of our garbage? It's impossible for someone to visit every house in a single night!"

But mysteries and unusual legends were what made any holiday special. Some parents chose to let their children speculate, others gave confusing explanations that only made the wondering wonder more.

"Everyone knows that there is no such thing as the Garbage Man," one boy told his brother. "It's the same garbage men and garbage trucks that pick up our garbage every week."
"No, it's not! How do you know??"
"A girl at school told me, her dad's a garbage man, so she knows. The garbage men take a month off in the summer, our garbage builds up, and when they come back they just go back to work. They work overtime and everything's gone by the morning."
"Oh, stop telling your brother things like that," their mother interrupted. "You used to believe when you were little. Even I still

LAST FAKE HAPPY WORLD

believe in the Garbage Man!"

The once bustling streets of the suburban city were growing silent. Dogs were indoors, cars were parked in garages, windows were boarded up with unsecure boards and fake nails. And there, on the dusk horizon of a nearby street, a filthy image soon rumbled into sight –
The throttle of an engine, the stench of burning rubber!
Like a junkyard dog, the rusty scrapheap car tore down the street, low to the ground with oversized rear tires, a ratrod of a vehicle with primer as its paint. Smoke bellowed from its exhaust as it raced and slowed, slamming the gas then slamming the brakes.
Awestruck eyes peered from the boarded windows of the houses it passed. The old monster car ignored all laws and jumped from streets to driveways, smashing through yards and sliding through trash. A trail of flies followed, swarming the streets as the car cruised on, rowdy music blasting from its windows.

"What do you think those stupid humans are doin' in those stupid houses?" Friday asked the Garbage Man, sitting in the passenger seat of the ratrod car.
"Same as always. They're sitting pretty," the monster told her. "Washin' their hair, washin' their dishes, scraping the slime off their ugly faces."
The Garbage Man was exactly as his name described, and somewhat close to how the holiday decorations portrayed him. A living manifestation of what you throw out, sculpted in a stocky bipedal frame. Wrappers, smashed pop cans, old vegetation and random items were held together by muddy sludge. Black eyes stared out as his garbage arms steered the old car, hardly paying attention as he skidded and swerved across the road.
Friday, on the other hand, was a human woman, filthy through and through. She was as attractive as a runway model, blue hair pigtails stained in grease and dirt. She wore patchwork bellbottoms

LAST FAKE HAPPY WORLD

that flared out like unwashed artwork, her lean upper body covered only at her disproportionately large chest, wearing a fur bikini made of raggedy blue stuffed animal bear heads.

The Garbage Man and Friday raced down the street with no regard. Flames shot out of the exhaust pipes, tires smoking and demolishing everything in their path.

"Look at all of these decorations this year!" Friday marveled, hanging halfway out of the passenger window. "Look at those inflatable pigs, how cute!"

"You kidding me? Those ain't pigs! Years back, people used to put out real pigs. You know, the real pork! Pigs of every color would be walking the streets in this garbage!"

"Ughh," Friday rolled her eyes, "you're so old fashioned, Daddy! Get with the times! No one has real pigs to put out anymore!"

The Garbage Man smiled his rotten smile and cruised slower, pointing at some of the things they saw, from decorations to old piles of collected trash.

"And look at these garbage 'cans.' All streamlined and blue, this one's the same as that one, the same as that one, the same as that one..."

"They are pretty stupid looking," Friday agreed, "like they're trying to make garbage look fancy, or futuristic."

"Where's the art, man? Garbage cans used to have a trashy style! Banged up and smashed-in sides, rust and every house had cans that looked different. What is this crap?"

The hotrod car veered from the street and knocked over a blue trash container, smashing it onto the bags beside it.

"How's a raccoon supposed to eat around here? He can't get into those closed-down lids like that! What a joke!"

"Whoa, whoa... What's that, Daddy?" Friday looked ahead and down the street, reaching over and tugging on the Garbage Man's sludgy arm.

"What, baby? I'm trying to drive over here! Hey, hey, you're right... *What do we got over here*??"

LAST FAKE HAPPY WORLD

The rusty car raced down the street, another vehicle coming towards them about two blocks away. As they drew nearer, anger began to well up inside of the Garbage Man.

"Don't get upset, Daddy," Friday tried to calm him as they approached. "I'm sure they know it's Garbage Day, they're going home right now…"

The garbage car slowed to a stop, the vehicle, a school bus, pulling up and then slowing to a stop as well. The Garbage Man and Friday stared through the dark slanted windshield, the school bus 'stop sign' extending out as children prepared to exit.

"You're tryin' to tell me that they don't know this is a freakin' holiday??" the trash monster complained, Friday biting her lip and holding onto his arm for support. "I've heard of some crap in my time, but this is something new! School on Garbage Day, of all days??"

Human kids walked cumbersomely across the street, in front of the bus and then in front of the idle car. They wore school athletic gear, a few wearing festive pig noses and looking curiously at the rumbling vehicle.

The Garbage Man revved his engine, both of his garbage hands squeezing the life out of the steering wheel.

"… Do it, Daddy!" Friday encouraged him, smiling wide with her sharp teeth. "Punch it!"

The children screamed as the Garbage Man plowed through them, flicking his middle trash finger out the window as the kids paved a bumpy path beneath the heavy wheels.

The holiday car stopped briefly, Friday opening the door and picking up one of the holiday pig noses from the bloody ground.

Back in and they sped off, momentarily dragging a few young people along and then none, Friday screaming laughter from the window along the way.

"Welcome to Cramp Burger, may I take your order?"
"Yeah, just give me whatever trash you're serving here."

LAST FAKE HAPPY WORLD

"... I'm sorry sir?" the voice from the drive-thru speaker replied. "Could you say that again, please?"

"Do you want anything?" the Garbage Man ignored the speaker and asked his girl.

"I don't know," she thought and pouted, unsure of what to order.

"Sir?" the voice prompted. "Could you repeat the order?"

"Calm down, man. I said give me whatever type of trash you're serving here. Empty out your dumpster in a bag."

"I'm sorry sir, but what are you ordering? Our dumpster? What are you talking about?"

The Garbage Man floored the pedal and drove around, slamming on the brakes as he reached the pick-up window.

"Sir, I couldn't understand – Oh, my God! What the hell??"

Before he could resist, the Garbage Man pulled the restaurant worker through the window, dragging him straight into the car and racing off.

"Got you, you little punk!" the Garbage Man laughed as he violently pulled at him, the boy's legs briefly hanging out through the driver's window.

"Let me have 'em, Daddy," Friday begged, taking the costume pig nose off and putting it on the worker, panic still coursing through his body.

"Oh, God, it smells like something died in here!" he cried out, in the pig nose and subdued now in the arms of Friday. "Holy crap, you've gotta be kidding me, are you the Garbage Man? The *real* Garbage Man?? This isn't a costume?"

"The real deal, buddy!" the monster driver told him, cruising down the road again.

"And that means that you..." the captive worker paused and looked to the girl that was holding him still. "Oh, Jesus Christ... You are so hot! You're Friday! You're so hot, I mean, you're filthy, but you're so hot!! I can't believe this!"

"You're a big fan of ours or somethin', buster?" Friday asked, running her dirty fingers through his greasy fast-food scented hair.

LAST FAKE HAPPY WORLD

"Then what'cha doing working on Garbage Day? Where's your holiday spirit?"

"Oh, I didn't wanna work, I had to, Ms. Friday! I swear! I love Garbage Day, I always have!"

"They made you work on my holiday?" the Garbage Man grew angry with such ideas. "Humans are ruining the magic of the season! School, work, what the heck's going on with the world now? It didn't used to be like this - Garbage Day is a day to throw it away, spend time with the family and throw your crap out."

"Look out!!"

The worker yelled as a bum stood in the road, a cardboard sign in his hands –

~ Happy Garbage Day: Need food. Anything will help! ~

The car swerved to hit him, the derelict rolling up the hood and over the top of the car, Friday laughing her head off.

"What the?? What's wrong with you??" the captive man cried. "You gotta go back! You might have killed him!"

"I hope I did!" the Garbage Man struck back. "What'd that sign say? Need food? Lazy bum, go dig in a dumpster!"

The rusty car roared and blasted fire from its exhaust, swerving and making hairpin turns, jostling the fast-food worker on Friday's lap.

"Look, I gotta... I have to get back to work, this is crazy..."

"What do you mean?" the Garbage Man asked back. "I thought you were excited to meet us?"

"I was, I mean, I am, but, but..."

Sweat dripped from his forehead.

"God, that smell," he continued, looking over his shoulder at Friday who just smiled back. "Seriously, it doesn't bother either of you? Like, it's really, extremely... rancid, just nasty. I feel sick..."

"Rancid?" the Garbage Man said and repeated back to himself, "Rancid. Remember that one, Friday. I like that, that's a darn good

LAST FAKE HAPPY WORLD

word right there."

"No seriously, I'm gonna be sick guys, like throw up sick, you know? You gotta pull over. You gotta let me out!"

"Say, you ever kissed a girl, guy?" Friday asked, looking around the side of his face at him.

"Kiss? Wait, what? Ughh, I'm telling you... I'm gonna throw up, what are you talking about??"

"Let me help you," the Garbage Man opened his rotten mouth and let out an intestine-scented belch, a drain fly exiting his throat along with it, filling the air with an additional layer of the lingering stench.

"Ughhh," the worker's stomach then gut-wrenched, set further in motion by the acrid humid aroma. "Ughhh... Blargggggggg – Blahhhhhhrggg..."

"Wheeee!" Friday laughed as their guest puked violently, playing with it like a child splashing in water. "You threw up everything! Get over here!"

"No, no!" he cried in teary eyes as she turned his head and forced him to kiss her, her long tongue tickling the back of his throat and forcing him to gag on additional vomit.

The Garbage Man laughed hard with his stinking breath, watching Friday kiss the man as he finally pulled away, barf all over his lower face as well as hers, dribbling down into her cleavage.

"...Ugh..." the man struggled to breathe and not dry heave, looking with alarm as Friday licked the meaty spit from her lips. "What is wrong with you?? That's freaking disgusting!!"

"What?" she asked and stared back at him with her beautiful eyes, his emptied stomach spread like frosting and soup across her chest. "I'm a big mouth, I eat anything. It was food when you ate it, wasn't it??"

The man struggled to get off from her, reaching for the passenger door in his sickness. Friday loosened her grip, allowing him to frantically open the door unrestricted. He stretched and fell out,

LAST FAKE HAPPY WORLD

hitting hard and rolling onto the pavement as the filthy car raced on. Down the street and away, the Garbage Man and Friday drove off and then were gone.

The restaurant worker limped down the quiet street of a neighborhood he didn't know. The intense absurdity of everything was striking him at once. Decorations that had seemed trivial now threatened to make him ill again. Brown lights, yard displays with cartoon rats and goats eating waste. Holiday music emitting from closed doors, rockabilly songs with the recorded sounds of squealing pigs. Everything, everywhere, was sickening at this moment. The piles and piles of trash, the stench of rotten waste. Stray dogs hunched over and defecating, flies festering everywhere and the nighttime air cooling the moldy trash, baked to a rot all afternoon underneath the summer sun.

And in that moment, as he sat sick on the curb and breathed in the stink of the street, the true magic of the holiday came to him. Garbage Day wasn't just one day out of the year. It wasn't just a holiday to throw lots of cool things out, or to take a bath with your family. It was present every moment in your life.

And that was something he would never forget. It was a lesson that he would share with his children one day, and a lesson that they would eventually share with their children too:

"Every day is Garbage Day on this filthy, stinking earth."

Black Baby

July 1986

The doorbell rang, and the Hooper family nearly jumped out of their seats, startled easily by the sudden sound.

"Pause the movie, pause the movie!" Marcia begged as she ran from the couch, grabbing the crisp twenty-dollar bill from the coffee table.

"Andy, get over here," Mrs. Hooper called to the family dog, the St. Bernard lumbering over to the couch. "Be a good boy."

Marcia opened the door and handed the money to the 'Jesus Pizza' delivery boy, Mr. and Mrs. Hooper sitting at the couch as the movie still played.

"Dad! Mom! You didn't pause it!" Marcia complained as she carried the large pizza with one hand, setting it down onto the coffee table.

"And where's my change, young lady?" her father asked, looking over his glasses at her.

"Duh, the tip?" Marcia said and asked at once, looking back at him in annoyance.

"She had to tip the delivery boy, Roger," his wife Monica reminded him. "They hardly pay those poor kids anything nowadays."

"A tip is fine, but that was a twenty-dollar bill! Do you know how much -"

"I'll get the plates, honey," Monica settled him, kissing him on the cheek. "Why don't you start the other one? This movie's kind of stupid."

"What??" Marcia complained as she grabbed a pizza slice from the box, completely annoyed by her parents. "But we didn't even get to the good parts! Why are we putting on the other one already?"

LAST FAKE HAPPY WORLD

"You heard your mother, she's the boss around here. I don't have to bring them back until Monday anyway, you can still watch it tomorrow."

Roger set the VCR to rewind the rented movie, 'CoolToDie World 2.' It was always a rough night at the video store on Fridays. Every new or major horror movie would be checked out, leaving these lesser known table scraps for the late comers to fight over.

"And here we go!" he sang in a silly voice, popping the tape out and pushing in the next. "The Jessica Chainsaw Massacre! What do you think about that?"

Marcia gave a thumbs-up, sitting with her legs folded on the floor and a mouth full of pizza. Andy the dog sat nearby, waiting in silence for anything to fall to the floor.

"Honey, we're starting the movie out here – Oh, and here you are! Welcome back!"

Monica came into the room with a balancing act. Plates, napkins and somehow even soft drinks were all held in her grasp at once. Her husband gave her a hand, setting everything up at the coffee table and then dimming the lights again, the movie just starting to get underway.

"What was this one called again?" she asked, putting a piece of the greasy pizza on her plate.

"The Jessica Chainsaw Massacre," Marcia answered fast, her eyes fixated on the television tube.

"Oh, that's right, the one with the box that your father kept staring at."

"What?" he blurted out. "I was? I mean, right, I was! I was trying to figure out who that actress was."

"Right..." Monica nudged him playfully. "It was sure difficult to recognize her, what with that outfit she was almost wearing."

"Are you guys going to fight through the entire movie?" Marcia moaned, looking back at them along with Andy.

"We aren't fighting, not yet anyways... Your father just has some

LAST FAKE HAPPY WORLD

wandering eyes, that's all."
"And wandering hands, if you're lucky!"
"Oh gross, Dad! Really??" Marcia cried and looked disgusted at her parents. "You're going to make me lose my appetite!"

Eventually the family settled in, Roger comfortably on the couch with Monica, Marcia laying on the floor with the dog. The rented movie was strangely wonderful, and at the same time, quite bad. There was murder, severed limbs and the constant roar of Jessica's chainsaw. It blasted from the speakers so loudly that Andy eventually left the room, choosing to sleep by his empty dog dish instead.

A bikini girl waving her chainsaw around, turning screaming teenagers into human cold-cuts. The Hooper family loved their horror movies, and the violent images garnered more laughter than terror. The movie played on into the late evening, and eventually Roger got up from his spot on the couch.

"Well, if you ladies will excuse the old man," he said as his stomach gurgled, "I need to pay a visit to the men's room."

"Too much information, Dad!"

"You want me to pause it?" Monica asked, the remote already in her hand. "It's almost over."

"No, no," he waved his hand, "I think I know how this one's going to end."

And as he left the living room, his stomach upside down from the pizza, he slowed down near a closet door. Peeking back down the hallway to make sure no one was getting up, he slowly opened it and reached blindly to the top shelf. Ah, there it was, his secret stash of naked girl magazines. With the top issue taken, and the closet door quietly closed, he headed up the stairs to the bathroom, reading material in hand.

"For Christ's sake, Carter!" he yelled as he rounded the corner, nearly stepping on the family cat's solid waste.

"You alright?" Monica called from downstairs, startling Roger to where he quickly rolled the magazine up, just in case.

LAST FAKE HAPPY WORLD

"Yeah, the cat missed the litter box again, I'll clean it up."

"*Carter*," his wife scolded the unseen cat from the living room. "You know, honey, he just gets out of his box a little too early sometimes."

"Mom! The movie!" Marcia could be heard protesting, the violent sounds of the Jessica Chainsaw Massacre roaring in the background.

Roger quickly scooped up the small dropping with a cat litter shovel and tossed it into the litter box. The scruffy brown-furred Carter came around the corner, just in time to peer into his box.

"It goes in there," Roger pointlessly explained to the house's resident feline. "You stay in the box until you're absolutely *sure* that you're finished. Understand?"

He gathered himself, realizing he was having a one-sided talk with the cat, and turned into the bathroom. With the light switched on, he closed the door and was ready for relief.

His stomach was turbulent. Something about the pizza and soda had upset it, and the uncomfortable bubbling feeling made sure he knew something wretched was going on in there. Seated at the toilet, he waited for his body to sort it all out, in the meantime turning to his secret reading material.

~ Centerfold Bold ~

He didn't think Monica would mind if she knew, and sometimes he suspected that she already did. But there was just something so tantalizing about it, believing he had a secret to privately enjoy. He looked at the issue he had blindly grabbed. Ah, the August issue, a few years ago. He knew it well and looked forward to seeing those August girls in all of their glory.

Roger's stomach twisted sharply, and he hunched over in pain. His eyes focused on the pages, forgetting about the inevitable bowel movement. Oh, these girls, these lovely, naked girls... With

LAST FAKE HAPPY WORLD

the familiar sights printed in these dirty pages, along with the arousing 'Jessica Chainsaw Massacre' still fresh in his head, Roger couldn't help but be turned on beyond belief. His stomach flip flopped while his relaxed mind fantasized. The pelvic stimulation and overturned bowels led to an eventual bought-upon and natural double relief.

"You missed the ending, Dad!" Marcia told him, the living room light back on, the VCR and television already off. "You have to see what she does to that guy!"

"Are you feeling alright?" his wife asked, looking concerned and putting her hand to his forehead. "You were in there for a while."

"I'm good, the pizza just didn't agree with me," he tried to explain, his adult magazine safely returned to the closet's upper shelf.

"Well, why don't you go on to bed. Marcia and I can clean up down here, you go lay down and relax."

It was easy to take orders from his wife, especially when they heavily benefitted him like this. His stomach felt fine after the bathroom ordeal, but no need to say that now. Going to lay down and relax was exactly what he intended to do.

Roger was in a half-asleep, half-awake trance when his wife came into their bedroom. She shooed Carter off from the bed, climbing in and snuggling up against her husband from behind. Pressing against him in her silk pajamas, his semi-alert self could tell that she was up to something.

"Stomach feeling better?" she purred at him, a sultry rumbling voice that she knew he couldn't resist.

"Mm-hmm," he replied with only sounds, eyes closed and facing away from her.

She kissed his neck, her hands touching at his body. Roger didn't move, enjoying this attention in his slumber state, though not quite as into it as he normally would have been. Monica's body was enough in itself to excite him, and she continued pressing it against his back, the thin silk sleepwear clinging to her shapes.

"I know you were all worked up watching that movie, you big weirdo," she teased, biting his earlobe. "Maybe you want to call me 'Jessica' tonight? Or I can chase you around the yard with a chainsaw tomorrow?"

"…Maybe," he joked, her attention coming on stronger.

Monica toyed with him and tried to work her magic, little by little realizing his body was being unreceptive.

"Roger…"

He laid there in silence for a few seconds, finally turning over to look at her in the dark.

"Did you already take care of yourself?" she bluntly asked him in an accusing manner.

"Did I what?"

"You know what I'm talking about! Did you?"

"Oh, come on…"

"Ah, so that's why you were in the bathroom for so long!" she joked, slightly annoyed and grabbing her pillow to hit him over the head. "Your stomach was fine!"

They shared an awkward laughter in their five-second pillow fight, interrupted by a sudden knocking on the bedroom door.

"Dad?" the voice of their daughter came from the hallway. "The stupid toilet is all backed up. I swear it wasn't me."

Monica's eyes went mockingly wide in the darkness.

"See? I told you my stomach hurt," Roger bragged triumphantly, grateful to the bad pipes and plumbing.

"Your father will fix it, sweetheart," Monica said through the closed door. "He's the one that backed it up in the first place."

"Gross…"

"Well, he is!"

With his beautiful wife disappointed in their bed, Roger made his

LAST FAKE HAPPY WORLD

way to the bathroom again, stumbling tiredly in his pajamas. It was a minor embarrassment to back up the toilet, but at this married stage in life he remained valiant and unphased. Into the bathroom, and he removed the dusty plunger from beneath the sink.

"What in the heck is this now?" he mumbled to himself, looking at the splashed water drops scattered across the seat.

The water level was normal and clean, so just to check he went ahead and pressed the handle. A clear flush. He waited for the water tank to refill and flushed again. The second flush and everything was working as it was supposed to. What was Marcia talking about? The toilet worked just fine.

"Fixed it," he announced as he walked back into the hallway, taking credit for it anyway. "Nothing your dad couldn't – HOLY CRAP! Jesus Christ, Carter!"

"What now??" Monica asked from the bedroom, Roger briskly walking in. "Did he miss the litter box again?"

"Oh, he did more than miss the litter box! I don't even think it was him! It had to be the dog, it's a freaking pile!"

"What? No," Monica didn't believe it. "Andy hasn't gone in the house since he was a puppy."

"Well, then come look at it! You tell me if Carter could crap that big!"

"Roger, would you just clean it up? I'm not getting out of bed to look at it. You're being ridiculous."

"You're arguing who crapped in the hallway now??" Marcia yelled across from her bedroom.

"… It wasn't the cat," Roger repeated quietly with a look on his face, going out into the hall again, ready to head downstairs and get a paper towel.

Monica sighed, sliding under the sheets and getting comfortable, the bedside clock already nearing midnight.

"And wash your hands after you – Oh, geez, what now?"

Roger was back already, standing with his arms opened wide in expression.

LAST FAKE HAPPY WORLD

"It's gone."

"What are you talking about? You're acting like you're drunk tonight, I swear that's the last time we order anchovies on -"

"No, really!" Roger explained with shell-shocked eyes. "It's like, really gone, off the floor! What the heck?! Do you think Andy ate it?"

"Roger, would you knock it off?" Monica sat up in the bed and shot him a warning glance. "First, the dog goes to the bathroom in the hallway, and now he eats it too? What is going on with you? Andy's not even upstairs, he's probably sleeping on the couch."

"Well, I can't sleep now," he said with his hands on his hips, "I'm wide awake."

"Good, then just go downstairs and let me sleep. Keep the dog company, make sure he's not eating his own 'you know what,' you weirdo."

"I swear, he had to."

"GOODNIGHT, HONEY," Monica interjected, sending him on his way as she turned over in bed.

Roger passed by the hallway spot in question, eyeing the floor where he knew he had seen a pile. Nothing, not even a stain. Maybe there had been something in that pizza after all, but he swore he wasn't seeing things.

He passed by his daughter's bedroom, the muffled sound of rock and roll audible from her headphones. Down the stairs, and past the living room he walked. Sure enough, there was the dog, fast asleep on the couch. Into the kitchen, and he poured himself a glass of milk, then looking around in the fridge. There was the Jesus Pizza box and its cold leftovers... He hesitated, and then took it with him anyways.

With pizza in one hand, milk in a glass with a straw in the other, Roger restarted the Jessica Chainsaw Massacre VHS tape. Andy snored alongside him as the television tube illuminated the living

LAST FAKE HAPPY WORLD

room walls, the chainsaw sounds playing at a low volume this late hour at night. With each snore, he couldn't help but look beside him at the sleeping dog.

"Andy, I know what you did," he whispered, setting his pizza and glass down at the coffee table.

Roger pried the drooling dog's lips open, looking at his teeth to see if anything looked suspect inside. Just the usual grime and spit. What could it have been, then? Perhaps he was seeing things after all, maybe a pile-shaped shadow, as stupid as that sounded to him.

On the television, the buxom Jessica brandished her chainsaw, blood splattering across her bikini-clad body. Roger relaxed and felt good, his eyes starting to get heavy as the clock approached 12:45am.

Shortly after, a smell woke him from his light sleep, filling his nose with a putrid scent that was completely unmistakable.

"That's it, Andy," he told the dog as he got up, blinking his eyes and becoming aware. "Come on, outside you go. And I thought *my* stomach was bad."

He led the St. Bernard to the sliding glass door, then out into the backyard. Though it had been threatening rain all night, there was still no storm, and Andy wandered off into the humid darkness as Roger slid the door closed again.

"Wow, does that dog stink," he said to himself, going into the kitchen and getting the air freshener.

A misty spray of the floral fragrance, and Roger returned yet again to the couch. Another failed attempt to watch this movie in its entirety, but he watched on nonetheless.

More bouncing bikinis, more gore and countless buckets of blood. It seemed strange to him as he watched, wondering why his wife and daughter liked this stuff as much as he did. He had met Monica at a horror movie convention, so she was warped before he knew her. But as for Marcia? The visuals flashed by on the screen as he pondered his method of parenting in a slowly sleepy manner.

But then that smell again –

"*WHAT THE HELL IS THAT?*" he quietly shouted, dragging out the sound of each word in a growing frustration.

The dog was outside, the cat was probably upstairs and everyone else was asleep. Roger got up from the couch and paused the movie, right at a scene where Jessica was topless, in the shower and washing the blood off from her chest. It caught his eye and he stared for a moment as he walked, heading to the light switch and then flipping it –

A black shape ran, fast and near the floor, rushing past the couch and quickly behind the recliner chair. Roger was too startled to speak or move, his eyes suddenly seeing Carter standing in a paused walk at the bottom stair. The cat's eyes echoed his same amazed expression.

"Did you see that??" he instantly asked the cat, Carter then stalking cautiously to the chair's side. "What was it? A rat??"

He knew that his house didn't have mice, let alone wandering rats. But it had to be something, a squirrel through the chimney or a baby raccoon. As he walked slowly toward the chair, his mind raced with the possibilities. Was it dangerous? Did it have rabies?? In the brief second that he had seen it, it was a blur of movement. Five, maybe six inches, like a boy's action figure, but thicker. Carter hissed now, making a low growling sound that reassured Roger he wasn't seeing things.

Both cat and man crouched, trying to look around the back of the chair, Roger unable to see with the shadows. The stench was horrendous, no doubt now that it was coming from this unseen animal. He decided to scoop up Carter and then carried him upstairs, walking softly and putting the angry cat into the bathroom. Whatever was down there, he didn't want it attacking his pets or giving them any strange animal diseases.

"You stay in here until I get rid of it," he ordered the cat, lightly touching it on the nose. "And stop that hissing, big shot."

LAST FAKE HAPPY WORLD

Before he left the safety of the bathroom, he grabbed the closest thing to a weapon he could find, the plunger from beneath the sink, along with a tiny flashlight. With Carter now closed in, he alertly headed back down the stairway.

The light was still on, the movie still paused at the revealing shower sequence, and Roger surveyed the living room like it was a crime scene. Andy was standing patiently in the backyard, up against the sliding door and looking in, but Roger waved him off. Not now. Now he was defending his house, his castle, against whatever sewer rat or possum had snuck in.

Plunger in one hand like a hammer, the small flashlight in the other, he crept towards the chair that the thing had run behind. He didn't want to kill it, whatever it was, but he at least had to see what he was dealing with. That terrible smell permeated the air, forcing Roger to breathe only through his mouth. A skunk, that was it, it had to be a skunk. An oddly proportioned, upright and bipedal skunk…

He got to his knees, nervous, and looked around the chair again. With the flashlight's tiny beam, he saw all the dust and crumbs unvacuumed behind it.

And stains.

Miniature, brown footprint stains.

He dropped the flashlight and panicked, quickly picking it up and shining its beam into the dark space.

A pair of tiny yellow eyes stared back at him, glowing behind the chair.

"Daddy."

Roger leapt to his feet and dashed back across the room, tripping over the coffee table and rolling off the couch, landing behind it with a loud crash. Andy was outside barking at the scene, Roger freaking out and clutching at his plunger.

LAST FAKE HAPPY WORLD

The stairway light came on, the rapid steps of Monica coming down to see.

"What are you doing down here?" she asked in a half scared, half annoyed voice, stopping when she saw the scene before her.

Roger's head peeked from behind the couch, toilet plunger in hand, the movie still paused at the scene of Jessica naked in the shower.

"You know what," she said, her arms folded at the randomness, "I'm not even going to ask. Let's just pretend I didn't see this."

Her husband was still too shocked to say a word, crouching behind the couch in disbelief.

"But will you at least let Andy in, so he stops barking?" she continued, turning to go up the stairs. "You're freaking me out tonight. And why is Carter closed in the bathroom? Good grief, Roger."

Monica continued to their bedroom, Roger still behind the couch. He waved at his dog through the sliding door again, signaling for him to hush and stop barking. There was no way he was letting him back in, not with this thing loose in the house anyway.

His eyes stayed locked on the chair, only looking away when he had to motion for the dog to stop barking again. 'Daddy??' Not only did he not know what it was, now he knew that it could speak! Or at least make noises that sounded like words.

And still that smell. Luckily, Monica hadn't noticed that, or maybe just decided not to say anything. Either way, he had some serious convincing to do when this was all said and done.

With a deep breath that he choked on and regretted taking, Roger gathered his courage for one more go at the chair. Stepping like a long-legged spider over the couch from the backside of it, he was careful not to make such a ruckus this time. Around the coffee table and past the paused movie, so nerve-wracked he didn't even glance at the naked Jessica, and back to that spot.

Here went nothing.

His flashlight in hand lit the way, the plunger poking behind the

LAST FAKE HAPPY WORLD

chair in tentative strikes. No sounds, no reaction. Another swing, another poke, still nothing. With as much courage as he could muster, Roger leaned and looked behind the chair, putting his face in danger of being bitten or maybe worse –

Face to tiny face, he saw the little figure and trembled in an extraordinary fear. It was the shape of a six-inch man, its entire body made of what looked like solid black feces. Time stood still as the two lifeforms stared in amazement at one another, its yellow eyes looking straight into Roger's unblinking gaze.

"...Daddy," it said again, an unmistakable boy's voice and not an animal sound. "Daddy."

"No, no, no," Roger answered back as he fell back, falling from his knees to his rear end, scooting backwards as the black creature began creeping toward him.

It stepped slowly, but Roger was panic-stricken and didn't know how to react. He got to his feet again and played keep-away, walking around the couch as the little fecal man cumbersomely pursued him.

"I have to be hallucinating, this can't be real," he tried to assure himself, looking for answers anywhere. "Or I'm dreaming. Please, please be dreaming."

"Daddy," the tiny thing said again, its little black arms reaching out like a baby.

"Please stop saying that," he begged the small monster. "Please, just stop talking... Crap! Carter, get out of here!"

The cat was back out of the bathroom, approaching the odd creature like a hungry tiger. Roger rushed to intercept him, nearly grabbing him by the tail as he managed to escape. There was growling, hissing and the little black monster ran off, beneath the couch and hiding as Roger at last gave up and fled to the stairway. This was far outside of anything he had ever dealt with, and he needed to regroup.

Up the stairs, down the hall and into the bedroom, quickly closing the door behind him.

LAST FAKE HAPPY WORLD

"Honey, you have to get up," he reached for his wife and shook her, his voice trembling. "You're not going to believe what's going on in the house."

"What are you talking about?" she asked with a yawn, looking up from her pillow and half asleep.

"Trust me, you need to see this, I can't believe what I'm seeing," he explained, taking her by the arm and nearly dragging her out of bed.

They stumbled together to the door, Roger opening it slowly and tip-toeing out into the hallway, the groggy Monica with her eyes hardly open.

"I was finally starting to fall asleep, you know."

"Just come with me, something crazy is going on."

When they reached the stairs, Monica stopped with a look of disgust on her face.

And there, slowly pulling itself up the stairway step by step was the black baby, Carter the cat just watching it from the living room floor.

"What the heck is that thing??" Monica cried in disbelief.

"Daddy," it called, putting a look of surreal shock on Monica's face as she quickly turned and fled.

Roger ran after his wife, both retreating into the bedroom and slamming the door shut, Monica leaping onto the bed.

"Tell me what I was just looking at!" she demanded. "What was that thing??"

"We're in the same boat here, I don't even know what -"

"And '*Daddy*?' It called you Daddy??"

"Yeah, that's a little weird, I agree -"

"We have to call somebody," Monica rambled on, hugging her knees to her chest. "Should we call the police?"

"And tell them what? That there's a tiny crap monster in our house??"

There was a faint, nearly unheard wet knock at the bottom of the bedroom door. Both husband and wife went silent, looking at each

LAST FAKE HAPPY WORLD

other and then toward the closed doorway.

"Daddy," came the small voice, muffled through the wooden door. "Daddy…"

Monica mouthed the word 'Why?' to her husband in question, Roger shrugging a terrified 'I don't know!' back to her.

They sat in wait a bit longer, hearing one more muffled 'Daddy' down the hallway before all grew silent again.

"It's quiet now," Monica whispered. "I think the smell's going away, is it still out there?"

Before Roger could speculate, Monica grabbed him by his pajama shirt. "Marcia! We have to get Marcia!"

"Her door's closed," Roger reminded her, "don't worry, she'll be ok. We just have to get this thing out of the house."

"How did it get in? I don't even know what it is, but how did it get in??"

Roger started connecting things together in his head, the little things from that night and a horrible theory began coming together.

"Oh, no…" he moaned, putting his head in his hands.

"What??"

"I don't know if I want to tell you. This might be the stupidest thing you've ever heard, but I think I just might have figured it out."

"…Well? Go on! Hurry up, that thing's out there in our house somewhere!"

He assembled his thoughts and laid it all out, feeling even more idiotic as he was saying it.

"Remember earlier, when Marcia said the toilet was backed up? Well, when I said that I fixed it, I was lying. It wasn't backed up anymore when I checked it."

"So? That doesn't have anything to do with this!"

"No, I think it does. Earlier, when I went to the bathroom – man, I can't believe I'm telling you this – I, um, made a 'solid waste.' And, as you would call it, I 'took care of myself' at the same time.

LAST FAKE HAPPY WORLD

Well, not at the *exact* same time, there were a few seconds of separation. But my point is, I flushed them together..."

Monica stared at him with her mouth hanging open in disgust.

"Why are you telling me this?" she asked, her mind completely repulsed by the idea. "We can talk about your bathroom adventures tomorrow if you want -"

"No, listen to what I'm trying to tell you! Something must have happened! When Marcia told me that the toilet was backed up, there was water all over the seat! Like something crawled out of it."

"So, what you're saying is..."

"Yes," he answered, not knowing what she was going to say next. "My reproductive fluids mixed with my excrement. In the toilet."

"This really is the stupidest thing that you've ever told me, Roger."

"Then you tell me. All I know is that there is a baby sculpted out of 'you know what' walking around this house like a horror movie, calling me 'Daddy.' Now I don't know what kind of supernatural biology we're dealing with here, but that little bastard thinks I'm its father!"

Monica was dumbstruck by the moronic notion. Supernatural biology? But what even made sense anymore now, being held hostage by a toy-sized creature of human waste. While her mind did somersaults, Roger was at the doorway, slowly prying it open and looking down the hall.

"Coast is clear," he called over to her.

"What are we doing? Shouldn't we have a plan?"

"You go to Marcia's room and tell her what's going on, I'll find the little guy and put him in a bag or something."

"How the heck am I supposed to explain this to our daughter??"

"I don't know," Roger answered as he stepped into the hall. "Tell her she's got a brother now. A little one."

"Not even funny."

LAST FAKE HAPPY WORLD

The married couple walked cautiously down the hall, Monica going into Marcia's room and closing the door, Roger passing Carter sitting beside his litter box.

"Keep your eyes open, Carter," he told the cat. "That guy's out here somewhere…"

The smell was present but not as strong. Roger made it to the stairs with the plunger in hand, and descended step by hesitant step. Poor Andy was now laying down outside, his head on the ground, still facing the sliding door. Roger decided it would be too chaotic to let him in now, but still there was no sign of the creature.

The living room, the kitchen, the hallways and the closet. A fast look over each area of the house came up with nothing, the putrid smell mostly gone now as well. With no success, he returned to the stairway, going up to the second floor and looking through the bathroom.

"Supernatural biology? Really, Dad??" his daughter startled him, standing in the doorway of her bedroom, side by side with Monica.

"…Yeah," he said, unsure of what to say. "Pretty cool, huh?"

"I don't think cool is the word that comes to mind, honey," his wife answered, her arm around Marcia. "Now our daughter thinks you're going crazy."

"Well, you saw it too, Monica. Don't act like this is just me!"

"Is that it??" Marcia cried, pointing at the floor behind where her father stood.

He turned fast and looked, Carter hissing as the small humanoid shape rose from the litterbox like a zombie from the grave. It was covered in the tiny pebbles of the litter, encrusting it like a miniature rock golem. Roger grabbed the growling cat away and dashed into his daughter's room, closing the door to hide with his family.

"Was that really him??" Marcia asked, relatively calm and sounding more excited than scared. "Was that the baby??"

"He's smarter than I expected," Roger speculated. "He must have camouflaged his odor by hiding in that scented litter. I didn't even consider that..."

"Oh, come on!" Monica went to correct him, grabbing the cat away from her husband. "Carter probably just buried him in there, that's what he's supposed to do. Right, Carter? You're a smart cat, you were just doing your job."

"So, is he my brother, or my half-brother?" Marcia wondered out loud, sitting at the edge of her bed now. "I mean, we have the same dad, but not the same mom. Who would his mom even be?"

"He's not really your brother," Monica informed her. "And we're getting rid of him as soon as we can."

"But does that mean Dad is his father *and* his mother? How can that be?"

"Daddy," the voice of the thing came from the hallway, all three family members staring at each other in silence.

"Whoa," Marcia said in astonishment, her first time hearing the voice, "that's creepy..."

"We really have to do something about this," Monica announced, trying to bring her family to a decision. "We can't keep that thing in this house, I don't care who it thinks its father is. Do you have any idea how unsanitary this is? He keeps walking around like this and we're all catching typhoid fever. Or pink eye!"

The voices of Monica and Marcia went on and on, Roger zoning out with the small cries of 'Daddy' periodically peppered in. He had to take control of this now, and he stood by the door for a long minute before turning the knob and preparing to open it.

"Honey?" Monica asked to no reply as the door swung open.

Her husband stepped out in a powerful stride, the small litterbox crusted figure standing in the hall before him. Like grabbing a toy from the floor, Roger grasped the small toilet-born baby with both hands and carried it off. Down the hall, into the bathroom from where it came, crying 'Daddy' the entire time.

Monica and Marcia followed, watching Roger hold the small figure above the toilet for a moment with one hand, looking into the glowing eyes of the creature.

LAST FAKE HAPPY WORLD

The drop.

The flush.

He let go of his would-be child, letting him fall like a dead fish into the swirling abyss of the toilet. But the supernatural baby held on, gripping to the seat as the water swirled and stopped.

"Flush it again!" Monica shouted and then quickly pushed the lever herself, a minor flush happening immediately.

"You have to wait! The water tank has to fill up!" Roger yelled back at her in frustration.

"Well, don't let it crawl out!" Marcia looked on nervously.

Thunder sounded in the distance, a storm approaching as they waited for the toilet to be ready. Monica ran outside the room and returned with the plunger, pushing the small baby away from the toilet seat so it fell into the water.

Another flush, and the pathetic creature spun in circles, the cat litter washing off from its fecal body. Its small frame smeared, but still no success.

"Do it again!" Monica directed her husband.

"It's not working! He's too big to go down, that's why it was backed up in the first place!"

Another rumble of thunder outside of the house, and Roger reached into the toilet bowl, the black baby's arms reaching up for the safety of its father's hands. As its wet body lay in his grip, he walked quickly out of the bathroom and rapidly down the stairs, his wife and daughter once again watching in pursuit. Through the living room and toward the sliding door, rain-soaked Andy still waiting outside to come in.

"Open the door, someone open the door!" Roger ordered as he neared it, Marcia running ahead of him and doing as told.

The door slid open and Andy ran in, shaking off the rain as Roger thoughtlessly threw the strange little person out into the storm. At last and finally, it was out of the house, the sliding door

LAST FAKE HAPPY WORLD

slammed shut.

Breathing heavy, Roger slumped to the floor, his back against the glass. His eyes were bloodshot, his thoughts barely able to process everything that had just happened.

"You..." his wife said and paused. "I'm sorry, but... You really should wash your hands."

He raised his eyebrows to show that he had heard her but said nothing. The stench remained, but it didn't bother him in the moment.

"Hey, Dad?" his daughter asked, her eyes looking to the glass door.

Roger turned to see, seeing the black baby's excrement hands up against the glass, sliding down and smearing in runny skid marks.

"Roger, what are you doing?" Monica asked as he stood up again, turning to open the door. "Don't let that thing back in here!"

But he didn't. He stepped outside and slid the door shut, picking up the small character and walking out a few steps into the rain.

"Daddy," it cried, its voice slightly muted by the rainfall pelting down.

Roger couldn't fully comprehend what it was or how it existed, but he recognized the same tone of a child calling for their parent. The rain struck it continuously, slowly disfiguring the tiny body in his hands. He looked at it with wonder, hearing its cries as the stool softened, wondering what he was supposed to do.

If it truly was his child, in some strange occult way, then the least he could do was hold it as it died. Lightning flashed across the night sky as the runny body of the black baby dissipated. All remaining features were flushed out, slowly sliding like a living-diarrhea through the fingers of its father.

Strange Birds

The school bus drove through the country roads, rolling hills and distant tree groves as far as the young eyes could see. Tommy's classmates sang songs that repeated lyrics over and over for the sole purpose of annoying. Though he sometimes joined in, he often trailed off and stared out through the dirty traveling window.

The sheer vastness of the country was incomprehensible to most grade school children. Tommy was accustomed to his pocket world of the same streets, same houses and exact same yards. These field trips away from school were his great escape and adventure.

Classmates had bragged of summer vacations to theme parks or the Grand Canyon, even places he had never heard of before. But not in his family. For him, every field trip to somewhere new was the journey of a lifetime, a place he could talk about at the dinner table, a new discovery out in the unexplored world.

Even if it was just to the circus.

There was nothing wrong with going to see the circus, in fact, Tommy was quite excited. But it was just a short drive an hour away from the school, another hour or so at the show, and then back to the doldrums of class again. Something about it lacked the normal thrill he felt when venturing out into the unknown. This trip filled him with the same feeling as going to see a movie. While it was fun, in his heart he wanted to be in what he watched, or even live inside of the show. Regardless of how dangerous it may be, snake pits and booby traps, that was the life he dreamt of as his eyes watched the landscape passing by.

The bus rolled along, the students inside still singing, some talking and the others throwing crumbled notebook paper at each other. Tommy sat alone, his empty aisle-seat sometimes occupied

LAST FAKE HAPPY WORLD

by a random kid moving up and down the bus, all to the dismay of their teacher and the chaperones. But no one in his class could ever obey or sit still that long, least of all on a break and field trip from those prison-like desks of their classroom.

Tommy watched as something new and interesting caught his attention, something in contrast to the rising and falling hills full of blooming flowers and towering trees. It was a cemetery, and he was both mesmerized and fascinated. Tiny crosses and giant stones elevated above the road as the bus passed by. His mind wandered and ran wild. Gloomy visions of all those coffins crammed in there, up against each other, decade after decade.

The road hit an intersection and the bus driver turned, still driving the road alongside the giant resting place for the dead. It rose up on both sides now, a pathway through the deceased and Tommy's arm hair stood on end. Now, this was exciting... This was already better than any thrill the circus would provide to his young adventurous heart.

He broke his gaze briefly, looking around to see if any of his classmates shared the sheer delight he was experiencing. No one. They continued yelling and joking and talking loudly, buzzing like insects in this honeycomb bus. He shook his head in disbelief and returned his face to the window, the road low enough now that he could barely see the gravestones at all.

Soon there was a stop sign, followed by another turn and the bus maintained a slow speed, then pulling into a gravel parking lot full of cars and other carbon copy buses. The circus tents drew the attention of his classmates, all rushing over to his side of the bus, pinning up against the windows and marveling at the brightly colored spectacle.

"Students! Back to your seats!" his teacher ordered everyone, resulting in a collective groan and disregard. "I mean now! Back to your seats!"

While most did as they were told, a pretty girl from class quickly

LAST FAKE HAPPY WORLD

sat in the space beside him, pretending she had been seated there all along. Tommy looked at her for a moment, her sight still set on the great circus tents on the other side of the window.

"Hi, Heidi," he greeted, ready for anything other than a pretty girl.

"Hey," she replied with no emotion or look, enamored with the visions outside.

Tommy looked to them and tried to feign excitement, not feeling the anticipation that no doubt Heidi had.

"They look like… giant spaceships," he awkwardly described, wishing he had stayed quiet immediately after saying it.

"They look like circus tents, you idiot," the pretty girl replied, shooting down his attempt at conversation.

He remained in silence, looking at her reflection in the window. At least she was sitting beside him, that would make today at least something to remember.

Everyone was instructed to exit the bus in an orderly fashion, and they did so until they hit the ground running, scattering out to the yells and dismay of their chaperones. Because they had been sitting in the shared seat, Heidi and Tommy had been partnered as a pair, forced to stick together and stay within the group.

While their classmates darted off in the general direction of the circus, Tommy's mind wandered back to the sight of that massive cemetery in the hills. It had been just along the road, so he figured that he should be able to see it, at least from a safe distance in the parking lot. With his teacher and chaperones distracted by the frantic bus-exiting, he carefully slipped around the parked vehicle, walking briskly across the parking lot.

"What are you doing??" Heidi called out to him, stopping and standing behind the school bus. "You're going the wrong way, stupid!"

Tommy brushed her off. "I'll be right back, don't worry. I want to see something."

LAST FAKE HAPPY WORLD

He walked faster, the sound of sneakers on gravel gaining as Heidi ran to catch up.

"We're supposed to stay together!" she said as she reached him, grabbing his jacket and forcing him to stop.

He looked at her and then past, looking to see if any adults were coming this way or watching.

Nothing.

"I just want to see something and then I'll come back."

He pulled away, stupefied that a pretty girl had *actually* just touched his coat, and continued across the dusty parking lot. The edge of the elevated cemetery was just ahead.

"Tommy!" she yelled. "I'm going back without you! You're going to be in so much trouble!"

He spun around in his walk and raised his arms halfway up, mouthing the silent words of 'I don't care.' And he did, but only a little. Being in trouble wasn't something he wanted any part of, but he couldn't resist the allure of this excitement.

Without looking back he continued, nearing a grassy slope that lay on the other side of the entrance road. Atop it would be that endless place of death...

Tommy quickly looked both ways, then crossing the street to the base of the incline. He calmed his nerves and set one foot onto the hill, ready to hike the short distance upward.

Almost instantly, the smell of cigarette smoke blew by on the air. It irritated his nose and watered his eyes, distracting him from his adventurous mission.

"I think you're going the wrong way, kid," a disorderly voice suggested. "Circus tents are back that way."

The interruption brought him back to reality and unsettled his heart. Alongside the grassy hill, standing at what looked like a four-foot tall sewer entrance, stood a man smoking a cigarette. He was a punk rocker, or something like one. He had a faded black mohawk, uncomfortable-looking piercings, safety-pins and tattered clothes. His face looked deathly, beady eyes like a bird with dark sleepless circles beneath his eyeliner.

"You want a drag of it?" he asked, offering the smoking stick from his dirty fingers to the child.

"... No," Tommy answered as he cautiously kept his distance. "I have to get back to my field trip..."

"A field trip, eh?" the punk asked, blowing segmented rings of smoke. "That's a cool trip there, going to the circus. You've ever been before?"

"No..." Tommy answered, standing still in the same place, half frozen in fear. "We had a carnival in my town, but I never went to the circus before."

"Yeah, it's cool, man," the stranger flicked the cigarette into the street. "What are you doing way over here then? You get lost?"

Tommy felt scared and took a deep breath, forcing himself to try and stay calm. "I just wanted to see, the um..."

"What, the graves? You want to see the dead people?"

To 'see the dead people' wasn't exactly what Tommy had been thinking. Hearing it that way, along with the man's alarming appearance, triggered even more fear inside of himself.

"Whoa, babe alert," the punk rocker broke Tommy's thoughts with a wave to the approaching Heidi. "This little beauty is your girlfriend?"

"Tommy! Get away from that guy!" she demanded from across the street, standing there in her summer dress.

"Don't freak out, babe," the man instructed her. "We're just hanging out over here, no worries! The name's Midway."

"I don't care what your name is, bum!" she ignored him with her sight locked on to her classmate. "Come on, Tommy! Get away from him!"

"Her name's Heidi," Tommy told him without thinking.

"What the – Tommy! Don't tell him my name! What's wrong with you?!"

"Ah," the stranger sighed, "so your name's Tommy and her name's Heidi. That's a cute pair of names for lovebirds."

LAST FAKE HAPPY WORLD

"What??" Heidi's face writhed in disbelief. "Are you kidding me??"

Tommy laughed at her disapproval, a strange bonding moment shared by the young boy and the stranger.

"You still want to see dead people?" the man asked, turning his attention back to Tommy.

"What the heck??" Heidi exclaimed, listening in astonishment.

"Yeah!" Tommy agreed, mostly doing so to shock his fellow classmate. How cool he must look to her, he thought, standing here and hanging out with this punk rocker.

"Then come on, dude," Midway gave a thumbs-up, directing a smirky sneer back to Heidi.

Without a word, Tommy went to walking up the hilly incline, heading toward the top and the beckoning tombstones. But before another step was taken, Midway halted him in his tracks.

"Whoa, whoa, where do you think you're going?"

"The cemetery?"

"No way, brother! The real show's down here, there's nothing up there but dead flowers and stones, man."

He motioned toward the low-clearance entrance, striking a match against the edge and lighting another cigarette.

"Tommy, you are not going in there! He's probably homeless, that's where he lives. He probably does drugs down there!"

"Relax, babe!" Midway shot her his continued smirk. "Go see the circus, go clown around with your friends. Tommy here wants to go on a real adventure, right, Tommy?"

Maybe he wanted to keep looking cool in front of Heidi, or maybe it was just the seductive word of 'adventure' that lured him in. But for whatever reason, Tommy took a step down from the grassy hill and toward the punk rock stranger.

"You cannot be serious right now," Heidi said in a dumbfounded tone. "You're really going in there? With him??"

Tommy looked at the strange man and then at his classmate Heidi. Who was she to tell him what he could or couldn't do? She wasn't really his friend anyway, she was only paired up with him today because she didn't have a choice.

"After you, young man," Midway held out his tattooed arm to invite Tommy in. "And you can run along, if you like. We'll be seeing you, babe."

Heidi marched across the empty street as Tommy descended into the entrance.

"Don't even think about touching me, you creep!" she ordered the man, standing near him to look down into the underground route. "Tommy? I can't see you… Seriously, this isn't funny! Get out of there! Tommy!"

And as she yelled into the blackness, Midway looked cautiously around to make sure nobody saw – Then shoving the young girl hard into the sewer-like entrance. She screamed, but it was lost in the echoing enclosure.

The mohawked man followed her in, closing a concealing door that all but eliminated any trace of an entryway. All three, the two young students and the punk rock stranger, were now closed away inside, hidden from the world and entombed beneath the massive cemetery.

"How long are you going to keep us here, you monsters??" Heidi cried and shook, her body shivering inside of a human cage. "We have families, you know! They'll come looking for us! And you're all going to go to jail when they find us!"

"All you do is squawk all day," a man in a dusty trench coat complained. "Don't you ever get tired? Don't you ever stop? Why don't you just shut up, like your friend Tommy boy here?"

Heidi said nothing and looked across at her classmate. He sat in a cage beside her with his arms around his knees, his jeans filthy from the clinging dirt. Neither had eaten a thing in the days since they were kidnapped. And now here they sat, standing and sitting

LAST FAKE HAPPY WORLD

in cages for what was next they didn't know.

It was like a miniature city down here, beneath the hilltop cemetery. There was electricity running from generators, rats and half broken arcade games. Midway was the first they had met, but there were other strange people that came and went from the tunnels in these dirt walls.

The one sitting in this room with the trench coat called himself 'King Fisher,' and he combed his blonde hair like seagull wings straight back. There were others they saw as well, passing through to other parts of the underground. Names like Roadrunner and Blackcap, Bluethroat and Whitethroat. Why they lived down here in the underground, they didn't say at first. But as the days went by, little things began to add up.

"Why aren't you feeding us?" Heidi asked, her voice strained from the severe dehydration. "I'm starving, Tommy's starving too..."

Tommy was still alive, though even at the mention of his name he refused to look up.

King Fisher conversed with some of the other punk strangers, ignoring Heidi's unending questions. They shared bad jokes and played music, playing those arcade games and living life like a party.

"They'll find us," Heidi helplessly complained to herself. "They know we're missing, they'll come looking for us."

"The parrot keeps repeating," King Fisher said and then called over to Midway, gaining his attention. "This little brat thinks her family's gonna find her, man. You believe that?"

The treacherous Midway smiled and bared his rotting teeth. "Listen to me, babe," he said. "Every year, kids go missing, it's no big deal, really. The world's a great big storm out there, and sometimes birds are gonna get lost in the storm, you know?"

"But why are you keeping us here??" she begged. "We didn't do anything to you. We just want to go home, right, Tommy??"

Her classmate tilted his dirty head a bit, his sad eyes looking through strands of unruly hair.

"Tommy, will you say something?" Heidi cried. "Tell them? Tell them to let us go home? I want to see my parents…"

The young girl broke down into sobs again and the gathering of strangers laughed. The underground party continued, though their apparent leader maintained his focus on the caged children.

"Do you really want to know what it is we do down here?" King Fisher asked, walking closely to the bars of their cages. "Are you sure that you really want to know?"

Tommy looked but didn't speak, Heidi leaned back in fear and kept quiet with heavy eyes.

"Do either of you know what a ghoul is?" the man with the blonde wing-like hair asked.

Heidi shook her head back and forth.

"Well then, let me put it in terms that even school children can understand. Midway – What do fish do in an aquarium when their fish friends die?"

Midway walked over to join his boss. "They eat 'em. First, they eat the eyes, then they eat their dead bodies and leave behind the skeletons."

"Right…" King Fisher approved, looking back and forth between the two cages. "And Toxy, what do vultures do, girl?"

The punk woman he called Toxy walked over to join the others, smiling with black lipstick.

"They eat the dead, kids!" she said with an off-putting sweet voice.

"Precisely!" King Fisher agreed, nodding his head in approval. "We're vultures, man. We're ghouls!"

"So, you're going to eat us?" Tommy finally spoke up, asking and speaking for the first time in the last few days.

"Not yet, Tommy!" Midway joked. "We're ghouls, not zombies, brother! Eating you alive would be in bad taste!"

LAST FAKE HAPPY WORLD

"Then why are we here??" Heidi pleaded, her hands gripping the bars. "You don't even need us! Let us go!!"

"Chill out, honey," the girl named Toxy came up to her cage. "We don't normally get real-life living people down here, still breathing and all. This is a real treat! Midway did us a big favor by going grocery shopping. We don't often get something so fresh!"

"You're just going to keep us down here until we die?" Tommy asked, calm from his exhaustion. "And when we die, that's when you're going to eat us?"

"That's the plan, man," King Fisher concluded. "It's just the food chain, kid, nothing personal."

A day or two more went by, and the children's bodies grew weaker. Tommy spoke now and then, Heidi all but giving up. New faces came and went from that punk rock hang-out room, no one offering food or ever even offering water.

"Hey, Tommy," the sweet voice of Toxy woke him from a starving slumber. "Midway told me that you seemed like a pretty cool surface-kid, back when he met you out there."

He looked at her without the energy to speak. She was the same as the other strangers, but almost pretty in a way his young eyes hadn't seen before. She dressed in unwashed yellow and black plaid-checkered pants, a black tank-top with suspenders hanging at her sides. Her makeup was black and smeared, her electric-yellow hair pulled up into two pigtail buns.

"You just gonna sit there and stare at me?" she asked, catching his sight. "Or you wanna spread those wings one last time?"

Tommy didn't answer or complain. He looked over to Heidi's cage and saw that she was still alive and sleeping, her chest rising and falling from her still-breathing breaths.

"We're not evil, you know," Toxy told him. "I mean, maybe we can't eat you alive, but we could just kill you and eat you right away, so at least we ain't like that, right?"

She unlatched the lock on his door and allowed him to slowly

LAST FAKE HAPPY WORLD

rise to his feet. His legs felt like rubber and he stumbled a bit first, then stepping slowly and was guided out from the cage by her hand.

"It's morning out in the world, that's when most everyone's sleeping down here," she informed him while assisting his weak walking. "Not that they would really mind, by now you're way too half-dead to try anything. My name's Toxic Canary, by the way, but you can keep on calling me Toxy."

She led Tommy on a brief tour of the underground, through the tunnels he had seen from his cage and to places he couldn't have imagined. It really was like a miniature town or a massive hidden mansion down here, doors to rooms and pathways around sewer waterfalls. A few of the punk rock ghouls were still awake, passing by with no alarm at his presence.

"Why are you here?" Tommy asked her, helpless and exhausted. "Why are all of you guys down here?"

"This is where we live, kid," Toxy guided him on. "This is where we have to live, really we don't have a choice. I mean, some of us live up on the surface. We live in alleys, under bridges and by railroad tracks, but this is the ideal life down here for us."

She helped him along, tiny steps at a time. They walked past broken glass and bottle caps, rock and roll posters and graffiti on slate rock.

"You wanna see something totally cool?" Toxy asked him, sounding more like a big sister than a flesh-eating ghoul. "Check this out – Pretty rad, huh?"

Up ahead in the wide tunnel was the deteriorating body of an elephant. It was half bone and half rotten flesh, its disintegrating trunk resting peacefully in the dirt.

"Incredible, isn't it?" she asked, poor Tommy never seeing an animal in conditions such as this. "The rats have been getting to it lately, but the circus buried it up there in the cemetery, so we dug it down. The thing was so heavy we thought it might be the 'World's Largest Man' from their freak show or something. Who would've

LAST FAKE HAPPY WORLD

guessed they'd be burying elephants up there now!"

"What do you mean," Tommy asked with slow-forming words, looking over the pachyderm head, "you dug it down?"

"Well, we didn't dig it up, silly! We live down here. When there's a funeral, and a new body six-feet deep, we dig it down. We'll dig in the ceiling until we hit the casket, bring it down and ration out our meals, then put the leftovers no one wants back inside that coffin."

"And then you put it back up?"

"Now you're catching on, kid!" Toxy gave him a shoulder hug, something strangely comforting considering the situation. "That elephant was just too darn big to put it all back up. We don't eat animals, but these rats sure do."

She took him past the rotten elephant corpse, the tunnels circling around until he had no idea which way they had come from. She showed him the spots of fresh dirt overhead, pointing at places where the most recent burials had been 'dug down' and then replaced. It was far removed from fun, but still something like an adventure with one of his kidnappers beside him.

"When I told Midway that I was taking you for a walk today, he asked me to bring you here, if I got a chance. I hope it's ok with you?"

Tommy didn't understand at first, being led through a stone door into a small tunneled room. Within it there were chopped up photos of fashion and hairstyles, all adhered to the three walls of dirt. A large mirror with lightbulbs was against the far wall, a chair set there and facing it.

"What's this for?" Tommy asked.

"Give me a sec and you'll see!"

It felt strange to have his hair cut into a mohawk. Tommy was still half out of it, but now back outside of the room with Toxy.

Today was so unusual.

LAST FAKE HAPPY WORLD

The friendliness of this girl, who would eventually be eating him. A new and wild hairstyle that his parents would no doubt ground him for, not that he would ever see them again.

Nothing was normal anymore, so he stopped asking questions. The heavy air felt cool on the shaved sides of his head, but without any nourishment, he still felt uncomfortably ill.

They continued walking until it became too much, and Tommy soon felt his eyes roll back into his head, his mind passing out as his legs gave out beneath him.

When he awoke, he wasn't in the tunnel he had last seen, nor was he back in his cage. Instead, behind dry eyes, he found himself sitting at a long empty table. All around him stood the punk rock ghouls in their various styles and strange colored hair. Tommy recognized a few, but the rest blurred together, standing huddled around the table he alone was seated at.

This was it. This would be death, and soon he would be eaten.

"Tommy," King Fisher's voice greeted him, stepping up to stand beside him, "your time as a prisoner has come to an end here. Both Midway and Toxy have told me such good things about you, but inevitably, your life is withering to die now. Tommy, I'm going to be frank with you."

He leaned closer, his beady eyes looking deeply into the child's, the others still standing and clustered around.

"When you die, possibly mere hours from now, I will eat your flesh. When I get full, my flock will divide up the meat I cannot finish, and together they'll peck your bones clean."

Tommy couldn't cry, he didn't care. There was only a spark of life left in him at this level of deprivation. His eyes fell in and out of focus, his fingers twitched, and his heartbeat crawled. He would be devoured, but death was his escape now, that final adventure coming soon.

LAST FAKE HAPPY WORLD

There was a thud on the long table, Midway tossing a limp husk up onto the filthy tablecloth. Tommy was unphased, his mind unable to concentrate and connect the things he saw with thoughts. His eyes left the shape, looking to Midway and then to the approaching Toxy.

"Do it," she said, making no sense to him. "I want you to do it, Tommy. Stay with us."

"And I want you to do it too, brother," Midway chimed in. "You seem like a really strange bird, man. Just like us!"

"I've been noticing that you've grown on a few of us," King Fisher added. "After deliberation, we've concluded that you'd make more than just a good meal, kid. We think you'd make an excellent addition to our committee."

Before Tommy and motionless on the dinner table, was the dead body of his classmate Heidi. Her face stared lifelessly like a dead fish and he stared back into her eyes, no emotion on his face. He didn't care, the ghouls around him wanted him to eat and be one of them, or to die and just be eaten. His young and now frail heart was pumping slowly at this edge of existence.

There was no choice. This human flesh would save his own. Without wait, he fed like a starving beast, wasting not, wanting nothing more than to live. This was Tommy's new punk rock reality, beneath the cemetery, down where the ghouls were playing broken arcade games and digging graves down. There was no Heidi here before him, there was no classmate here from school. Now, there was only death's gift of life-giving meat.

"That's our boy, Tommy!" King Fisher shouted with pride, putting a father-like arm around him. "Welcome to your new home, kid!"

And for the first time in his life, Tommy not only felt accepted, he felt like he was living the adventure. All of those boring days in school were over, and all of his worries simply flew away as yet another bird was lost in the storm.

Post Traumatic Halloween Disorder

A push-up bra beneath the revealing pink dress top. A small crown-tiara set into full, beautiful blonde hair. White platform shoes, white thigh-high stockings and a low-cut pink skirt of a dress. Pink glitter everywhere, and thick makeup too.

"I thought we were dressing up as King and Queen?" Mickey asked his girlfriend. "You look like a hooker."

"I do not!" Calliope cried back in shock, looking down and carefully studying her Halloween costume. "This is a Princess dress, Mickey!"

"Then why's it so slutty? Everyone's gonna see your stuff."

"It is not a *slutty* costume! The box called it a 'Bimbo Princess' costume. This is how women dress for Halloween, it's perfectly acceptable to normal people!"

Mickey shook his head and turned his attention back to the television. On screen was a pre-game show for the World Series.

"What are you doing??" Calliope walked in front of the broadcast. "We should've left for the party half an hour ago!! You're not even ready!"

"I've been ready!" he barked back, taking a costume crown from the armrest and putting it atop his disheveled hair. "See? Here's your handsome King."

"What about the costume I bought you??"

"I'm not wearing all that," he complained without making eye contact. "It looks goofy. Besides, I'm just gonna be watching the game over there anyways, who cares?"

"I care about it, Mickey!" Calliope complained, fighting back the makeup-ruining tears in her eyes.

"I'll wear the crown, and that's that. Besides, everyone's going to be too busy looking at your half-naked body to even notice that I'm there."

The car ride to the party went better. The Halloween decorations,

LAST FAKE HAPPY WORLD

the children trick or treating, the crisp fall weather – Everything that made Halloween magical was in effect. Mickey drove, Calliope watching through the passenger window at the world of fun around them.

"Look at these costumes!" she cooed with a shining lipstick smile. "Aww, look at that little guy! He's a werewolf!!"

"If any of your students see you dressed like that -"

"They wouldn't even recognize me!" she interrupted. "I don't dress like this when I'm working, Mickey. Geez! Besides, is that any way for a King to speak to his lady??"

The low sound of the baseball game played on the radio, no answer given.

"Mickey, come on!" Calliope moaned and gave him a playful shove. "It's Halloween! Can you turn that off??"

"Really? It's the World Series! This is bigger than Halloween! Do you realize that if -"

"Dragons!" she interrupted him again, pointing out the window at devil-costumed teenagers walking down the sidewalk. "Protect me, my King!!"

"Oh, man," Mickey rolled his eyes at her silliness. "Yeah, yeah. I'll protect you, Calliope."

She reveled in her quick attention-winning victory, hugging her boyfriend as he drove on. "Look! There are, like, sooo many monsters and demons on the prowl... We have to defend our kingdom."

Calliope looked at Mickey and then paused, waiting for him to continue her made-up storyline.

"Mm-hmm," he agreed. "Lots of monsters."

"Mm-hmm," she mimicked his masculine voice back with a nod. "Because if we don't?"

Mickey was silent for a few moments.

"You know the umpire in this game better not -"

"Mickey! Come on!!"

LAST FAKE HAPPY WORLD

The party was a modest sized get together of mutual friends, familiar faces and a few semi-costumed tag-alongs. They arrived late and last, as usual, with Calliope as the only one there in such an outgoing outfit.

"I thought this was supposed to be a costume party??" she complained to another woman who's name she didn't know.

"Um, it is," the woman replied with a hint of disgust. "I'm a cat." Thin, eyeliner lines decorated the lady's cheeks as hard-to-see whiskers.

"A cat? Where are your ears?" Calliope asked without trying to be rude. "And no tail?"

"*She's a cat*," another woman walked up and repeated, looking at Calliope's costume in complete disbelief. "You're dating Mickey, right? Aren't you a teacher?"

"I am! Actually, I'm a substitute teacher."

But as she talked, the pair of women walked off, leaving the conversation and Calliope standing alone.

As she headed through the kitchen and towards the den, small conversations stopped uncomfortably as she passed. She distracted herself and her increased uneasiness as she looked for Mickey, following the sounds of the television to find the love of her life.

"Darling!" she blew into his ear and leaned over the back of the couch, hugging him and kissing him on the cheek. "What are you doing?"

"Top of the 2nd," he said, his eyes staying with the broadcast, "bases loaded, and they walk in a run. Can you believe it??"

"No way!" she played along as if she cared, looking around at the other men watching the game. "Ok, well... Come see me when it's a commercial... Or something."

Calliope walked back towards the kitchen area she had just left, taking bat-shaped cookies and a cup of blood-red punch. It was starting to feel strange, being here as a couple but standing alone. Most of these people were only Mickey's friends anyway, and the few she would've talked to, she didn't see around.

"That's a nice costume," a voice cut in. "What are you supposed to be?"

It was one of the guys who had been watching the ballgame, now standing eagerly with his attention set on her.

"Um, the box called it a Bimbo Princess costume," she answered uncomfortably, the stench of liquor on his rancor breath, "but I'm supposed to be a Queen."

"I like it!" the man over-enthusiastically replied, his eyes slowly climbing from her legs to her chest. "Sort of like a sexy cartoon, you know?"

He made a point to stand uncomfortably close, his jean legs bumping against her thigh-high exposed legs.

"You're the girl with Mickey," he said, his glance heading back down. "You guys serious?"

"Yeah, we're pretty serious… Like, super serious."

"Oh, that's cool, real cool," the man went on. "Say, you wanna come see my car, maybe go for a little drive? Mickey's in there watching the game still, so…"

"I'll be right back!" Calliope quickly replied, looking for any excuse to leave. "I need, um, a cigarette."

She didn't smoke, but automatically walked toward the smell of cigarettes through the kitchen's back door, toward the patio. Her uneasiness at this party was pushing past her limit, her revealing costume fittingly making her feel overexposed. She pushed open the screen door and stepped into the hazy smoke-air behind the house.

"… And then she shows up with him, dressed like a whore?"

Calliope froze in her tracks, then taking slow steps out onto the unwelcoming patio.

"Oh!" the unknown woman panicked when she saw her. "Hi, Calliope! We were just talking about that movie that came out."

The woman continued her lie, a fake conversation between the women outside about a movie that obviously didn't exist. Calliope

LAST FAKE HAPPY WORLD

didn't participate in the talk or smoking, instead just standing there as a nervous wreck and unsure of what to do.

"Ladies!" came the voice of the same man from inside, the screen door opening as he came out to join them. "Any of you girls ever smoke a cigar?"

His hungry eyes stared Calliope's body down as she walked briskly past him, grabbing the door before it closed and returning to the house. She power-walked past the cat-costume girl and a few others, hurtful words bouncing off her ears like 'who does that?' and 'what's wrong with her?' By the time she reached the baseball game in the den, tears were already running down her cheeks.

"You know that I have these problems!" Calliope sobbed to her boyfriend on the car ride home.

"Yeah, trust me, I know. But you don't have to embarrass me in front of my friends like that! We weren't even there for an hour."

"I didn't do anything wrong! I tried to be friendly, but they hate me!"

"Why do you always say that? Nobody hates you," Mickey told her, the baseball game now in the 6th inning on the radio. "My buddies were even telling me how hot you were."

"Yeah, I bet they were. One of them was trying to hit on me!"

Mickey said nothing, his attention suddenly focused on the play by play commentary.

"Did you even hear me?" she asked in a lighter voice, holding back the constant tears.

"Dammit!" he yelled, startling her. "How do you blow a lead like that?? You don't pitch to him!"

"You aren't even listening to me!" Calliope wept. "You don't even care!"

"What?" he asked, realizing he didn't know what she was talking about.

"I've been looking forward to Halloween with you all year, and

LAST FAKE HAPPY WORLD

you haven't even been paying me any attention!"

"Aw, come on, babe," he hurried and tried to charm her. "Come on... Hey, look at all these monsters out here, huh?"

She pouted and refused to talk.

"We have to protect our kingdom, right, Queen? Yeah! Look at these monsters! Whoa! We better get back to our castle and make sure it's still there!"

Calliope couldn't help herself but smile just a fraction, Mickey's right hand then resting on her leg.

"Maybe when we get there," he said in a mock-serious voice, "we can, you know, check on the royal bed chambers?"

Calliope grinned, scrunching her wet eyes in pretend anger at him still.

"And keep that costume on," he added. "I think I'm starting to like how it looks on you."

Back home and Calliope sat alone in the bedroom, the lights low and the door open, waiting for Mickey. She tried to look seductive, laying in her costume with an alluring pose, growing impatient as the minutes passed by. What was he doing? It was too late for trick or treaters this time of night, and the baseball game had to be over by now.

Finally giving in, she reluctantly got up from her bedroom pose and walked into the upstairs hallway, seeing the illumination of the television from the stairway.

"Mickey?" she called out as she headed down. "Are you coming to bed?"

"No, not right now," he coldly responded. "Would you believe they're in extra innings?? These idiots are really throwing it away now!"

There was something in his voice that showed his utter disregard. Calliope felt it, the horrible letdown of a day now at its peak. He paid her no mind, his crown-wearing silhouette sitting there so carefree, watching the World Series as if his girlfriend's feelings

LAST FAKE HAPPY WORLD

didn't matter. She had always tried to accept his hobbies in the past. But if it wasn't this, it was something else. There was always a distraction, and there was never time for her.

"Do you still care about me?" she asked him with an unplanned and dramatic voice crack.

"Oh, not this again... Are you kidding me??"

He didn't look back at her, so she stepped in between him and the television. His face lacked compassion, showing an unhidden resentment just below the surface.

"Calliope, darling, this is really not the time for us to have that talk," he spoke down to her. "Go upstairs, go to sleep, you'll feel better in the morning."

She stood her ground, blocking the World Series with her body, waiting for him to answer her question.

"Would you fricking move??" he yelled out. "It's not enough that you dress like a hooker on Halloween, now you have to act like a baby too? What's wrong with you??"

She began to cry hard, Mickey getting up from the couch in what she anticipated was a hug, instead moving her out of the way so that he could see the game.

"Just stop it already, would you?" he reprimanded her. "If you're gonna cry, go in the other room or something. I'm trying to watch the game."

"You don't love me anymore," she sobbed with her makeup in a black mascara mess. "You wish I would just kill myself."

"And now this stupid 'kill yourself' crap again. Nobody cares, Calliope. Yeah, right, kill yourself. Nobody cares, your life is *so* difficult."

She cried harder, heading away from the television and away from her boyfriend.

"Go to sleep," he yelled as she shuffled up the stairs. "You're not killing yourself, stop acting stupid."

LAST FAKE HAPPY WORLD

That night, Calliope slept deeper and in a stranger way than she ever had before. A bottle of sleeping pills, passed out, trying to die and an attempt to escape her conquering depression.

She dreamt of Kings and Queens, kingdoms being attacked by child-size ghouls and ghosts. She saw herself fending them off, killing all the werewolves and slaying every frankenstein, dressed in her Bimbo Princess costume. 'Protect our kingdom' was all she could hear, 'protect our kingdom,' over and over.

When Calliope finally awoke, she found herself in a hospital bed, her brain punching against the walls of her skull. This was where she spent the next few days - All alone and without visitors, no family that knew, no family that cared.
Mickey was out of the picture too, never seeing her again and moving on in his life. She had attempted and ultimately failed to commit suicide on Halloween, and now was left utterly alone, winter on the horizon with a new depression too.

Calliope spent the next few months in and out of counseling, recounting the events before and after her attempt. She spoke of old boyfriends and poor family relationships, where she had been before and where she was heading next.
When the spring and summer came, she finally began to feel like herself. She was moving on past Mickey, building herself up and feeling confident again. By the end of summer, she was cleared to substitute teach once more.

And then October came.

The decorations, the themes, the over the top displays at stores and the all-around atmosphere had a strange effect on her mind. She hid it well - Listening to students bragging about what they were going to dress up as, watching scary movies and acting as if she felt as normal as could be.

But somewhere in the recesses of her mind, the brain damage was waiting. The days ticked down towards Halloween, Calliope's eyes seeing things differently as the anniversary of her horrible holiday approached.

"Ms. Sweetcheck?" one of her 'for-the-day students' asked. "Are you going to dress up as anything?"

Calliope looked at him blankly. He stared awkwardly, waiting for a response.

"I don't know," she finally answered, sitting at the desk. "What are you going to be?"

"A vampire," he told her, a proud smile on his ten-year-old face.

"Ooh, a vampire! That sounds scary!" she replied with pretend terror. "I think you'll make a really frightening one…"

Calliope paused, wanting to say his name but not able to remember what it was. Substitute teaching wasn't an easy job, and she seldom saw the same students, but still she usually tried to at least learn their names for the day. For some reason, her brain just couldn't focus right now. Michael? Mark? Something with an 'M.'

The school bell had already sounded, and she watched him run away, out through the door with the other students and now she remained in the classroom alone. Her mind went adrift with strange visions and ideas. It was like a movie, she daydreamed about Kings and Queens, castles and kingdoms. And for the first time since her suicide attempt nearly a year ago, a boiling rage and anger built up inside.

"Say, Ms. Sweetcheck?" an older man's voice came into the room. "Calliope? Is it alright if I call you that?"

She pulled herself out of the trance, looking vacantly at the school's principal.

"Thanks again for coming down here on such short notice this morning," he told her. "The kids seem to love you, everyone seems to love you."

She saw his stare at her buttoned-up blouse, a bead of sweat at

LAST FAKE HAPPY WORLD

his balding hairline.

"Of course, Mr. Lynott," she replied, overlooking his hungry eyes. "I'm happy they accepted me so easily."

"Who wouldn't!" he instinctively wiped the sweat away, another bead forming to replace it.

Calliope smiled and got up, gathering her school materials and purse, Mr. Lynott then asking a desperate last-minute question.

"Say, before you leave, you wouldn't happen to have any plans tomorrow, would you? For Halloween?"

The word Halloween on his lips rang in her brain like an alarm clock. It was already here, tomorrow was the day. It had been creeping up on her all year like a monster, and now, so soon, it was ready to attack.

"I'm sorry, Mr. Lynott," she replied and advanced towards the classroom door. "I can't remember exactly what, but I know I have something I have to attend to."

He continued talking as she walked, his voice blurring with the growing noises that were spinning in her head.

The day was here, one year after the nightmare. Calliope was stirring in the quiet house, humming unusual songs as she prepared for the demons of Halloween night. The sun was dropping, memories of a distorted yesterday crossing into a misinterpreted vision of today.

Something was changing in her brain. Her stomach growled from skipping dinner, and she found herself painting one of Mickey's left-behind baseball bats. It was now a pastel pink, Calliope then spreading out various pieces of shiny jewelry on the floor. With a maniacal smash, she pounded the bat over and over until the stones imbedded in its dripping wet-paint wood.

"A royal scepter!" she presented the weapon to herself in a cute voice, her eyes far off and her lips holding the smile unnaturally long. "I know they're almost here. We have to hurry to protect our kingdom."

LAST FAKE HAPPY WORLD

Darkness was descending on the city. Behind her closed door, Calliope was almost prepared for a night unlike any other. She donned her revealing princess costume once more, not just wearing it but believing it. She painted her white face white, a blonde wig over her blonde hair. Heavy makeup, shining lipstick and handfuls of glitter across her showcased body. With her baseball bat scepter in hand, she was ready for Halloween this year.

Costumed children rang the doorbell, but it was too late. Calliope Sweetcheck was already gone.

Autumn leaves blew across suburban streets, children running from door to door. The air was mild with a wind, carved pumpkins inviting trick or treaters to carelessly revel in the night.

Little zombies, skeletons and witches made their way down darkened sidewalks and unlit driveways, some alone and some in groups, some with parents or running ahead. Calliope walked alone with her disarming smile, setting off on her violent mental crusade.

Growing boys did double takes as they saw their first glimpse at a woman in thigh-highs. Accompanying fathers did the same, eyes nearly falling out of their heads at the sensual sight of such a body and costume combination.

Calliope walked seductively beneath the dim yellow street lights, hyper aware with her royal scepter gripped madly in her hands.

Beneath the shadows of a tree, on a quiet sidewalk of a quiet street, an adolescent mummy walked alone. With the costumed child's eyes and hands rummaging through his candy bag, a swift swing of the baseball bat cracked his fragile skull. A drop and thud as the lifeless body fell to the shadowy pavement.

Calliope breathed a sigh of relief. That was *easy*. Her brain had worried that these monsters would put up a horrible fight, but here one fell already, blood seeping out into the darkening mummy wrappings. She smashed its evil body once more for good measure,

LAST FAKE HAPPY WORLD

a slight twitch and then it lay still.
   One down...

   She patrolled the streets of her kingdom with alarm, so many of these small demons were spawning, banging on locked doors and demanding nourishment. Some pretended to be friendly, waving and playing, even traveling in groups that for now she held off on.
   Dark streets and alleyways were where she found most of her early success. Bones broke beneath her royal swing, skulls were smashed in and jaws shattered. She killed two werewolves and had to chase down another, pinning it beneath her kneeling legs as she pounded the scepter into its septum.

   Dealing out death felt grand. With every vertically-challenged devil she slayed, her kingdom would be safer. But the night was still young, and there were many more monsters yet to slaughter.
   A small coven of short witches paraded down the road. There were four of them, going door to door and cackling laughs of joy at the hexes they were no doubt bringing. Calliope stood across the street, watching as they carved their unholy path onward.
   "Say, uh, you're a little old to be trick or treating, aren't you?" a man's voice called from an approaching shadow. "But I like your costume. A little risqué for the kids, though. Not that I mind, of course!"
   He was taller and more human than the other monsters, a friendly demeanor, but Calliope still couldn't be too reckless - Not with those powerful witches just across the street.
   "Who are you?" she asked, an offsetting look displayed upon her face. "Actually, what are you?"
   "Why, I'm a *mad scientist*," he bragged with a poor pose, raising his bushy eyebrows as if to impress her. "That's my daughter and her friends over there."
   Calliope studied his outfit quickly. Dirty smock and apron, a belt with multi-colored test tubes, goggles and wild white hair. There

didn't seem to be anything he could fight back with, but she weighed out her options of this confrontational old man.

"One of those witches is your daughter?" she asked, eyes back and forth between the miniature coven and the man. "And you're ok with this?"

"What?" he responded with an odd look. "Sure, I mean, I'm a mad scientist after all, right? Experiments and making monsters, what's a little witchcraft in the family?"

Calliope swallowed hard, knowing this scientist would have to die. But so near these tiny witches, she had to pull him away.

"I want you to come with me," she told him in a rushed idea. "Let's go somewhere."

"Come with you?" he asked, his tan face turning red. "Oh, man, I wish I could... I kind of have to keep an eye on the kids."

"I want to be alone with you," she said and pushed up against him, pressing her hand against his leg. "Just for a minute, I'll be fast."

"Dad??" a high-pitched voice called out from across the street, a few houses down.

"Don't worry, sweetheart!" he nervously yelled back. "I'm just catching up with a friend of your mother's! Go on ahead, I'll be along in a minute!"

Calliope stayed out of sight in the shadows, then taking the mad scientist's hand and leading him in between tall dark houses. Here, in privacy, his true nature was seen. The man's hands went all over her body, grabbing and feeling everything at once like a neglected lover. Calliope pressed him off.

"Easy, mad scientist," she said playfully. "Tell me, do you love your wife?"

The man stood uncomfortably in the darkness, hesitating before confessing.

"...Yeah, a little bit," he admitted. "Does that matter, though?"

"Is she also a witch?"

He nodded, easing up his tension. "Sometimes she can be a bit

LAST FAKE HAPPY WORLD

of a witch..."

"Well, then this will have to be our Halloween secret," Calliope comforted him, a strong grip on the baseball bat scepter. "Close your eyes for me, pretend that I'm your witch wife..."

The mad scientist stood there, turned on with his guard down, eyes closed with his lips puckered up.

Calliope swung the bat into his face, a broken howl through his pulverized teeth and blasted mouth. He tumbled to the ground in inescapable pain and she mounted him, bashing his stubborn body that was slow to die until the very end. The blood splashed on her fingers and dripped onto her dress, the man's body laying lifeless as she triumphantly came to her feet.

Another one down.

Calliope skipped like a young girl as she continued patrolling through the neighborhood. Little by little, she murdered more costumed children in the shadows of the night. Teenage boys in ghost costumes followed her and vanished, teenage girls dressed like skeletons lay with their real bones bent and broken. Her stomach rumbled approvingly as she ate their collected candy, sucking suckers and chewing their gum.

There were scarecrows, gargoyles, aliens and evil clowns. All through the town, Halloween was painted red. Young bodies were piling up in the unlit doorways and dark backyards, the disturbed Calliope Sweetcheck massacring as many of the monsters as she could.

A car with tinted windows pulled up alongside her, slowing to match her pace.

"Hey there, gorgeous..." a man greeted as the passenger window slowly rolled down. "Where's a girl like you headed?"

Calliope waved and continued to skip forward. "Got work to do," she exclaimed, eyeing the vehicle's occupants.

A vampire sat behind the wheel, a low-level demon sitting in the passenger side. The backseat she couldn't see.

"I bet you do..." the passenger demon responded. "Say, you wanna go to a party with us?"

A party. Calliope stopped skipping and stood beside the car door, the word reverberating in her head. It hurt, though for some reason, it also made her grin.

"Maybe I do," she answered, staring strangely. "Will there be monsters like you guys there?"

"Yeah, yeah," the driver told her. "It's Halloween, isn't it? Come on, get in!"

He motioned to someone in the backseat and the rear door opened, a light fog of cigarette smoke rolling out into the street. In the back of the car sat two ugly demon men, their eyes dry-red and their clothing in ripped tatters. Calliope climbed over and between them, ready to kill at any time, the car speeding off into the evil night.

"It's just down the street," the passenger looked back and told her. "Wow, you're really something."

"I like your costume," one of the backseat demon boys told her. "Whoa, this blood looks real, man!"

"Yeah?" Calliope asked, staying alert and ready. "It tastes real too! Lick it!"

She took her hand and placed a finger on the boy's lips, the blood of children still fresh beneath her fingernails.

He looked nervous being put on the spot, and then tasted her finger-tip anyway, his eyes reacting to the thrill.

"Oh gross! It really does! This girl's awesome!"

"I bet she knows how to party, too!" the other backseat demon chimed in. "You wanna get wild tonight?"

"I think I wanna go *crazy* tonight," she outdid him, overpowering the boy's bravado.

"Easy back there, guys," the vampire driver interrupted. "My car, my girl. Got it? No one lays a finger on this chick before I do."

Calliope disregarded the salacious remarks and waited. These

LAST FAKE HAPPY WORLD

were simple monsters to her and she expected nothing less than monster behavior. The car ride was swift, pulling to a curbside just ahead of a forest preserve, everyone then exiting out.

The vampire put a strong arm around Calliope's thin waist, walking with his small group into the woods and near a faint sound. There was a small, hidden bonfire within. A gathering of teenage monsters partied, drunk on drugs, wasted and passing out. There were topless devil girls and werecats, werewolf boys and someone that looked like the devil himself. A radio played rock and roll, Calliope feeling as if she had stumbled upon a den.

"Welcome to the party!" one of the demon-boys told her, then joining the small crowd of revelers.

"Make yourself at home," the vampire suggested as he began to follow his friends off. "I'll get us some drinks, then you and I will get our own little party started."

Calliope gave him pretend hope with an empty wink of her eye, staying in the shade of the trees as she watched the boys melt in. This was even better than expected. Creatures of various races and natures, all mingling and fornicating, ripe for the royal slaughter.

"Hey, baby," the vampire already returned. "I got you a beer, no charge this time."

"Wow, so sweet!" she lied and held the unopened can.

"That's right," he bragged, drinking his own in one long chug. "You stick with me and you get the special treatment. Now why don't you and I get to know each other better?"

"Aren't you an evil little monster?" Calliope widened her gaze and dropped the unopened beer can. "Why don't you close your eyes for me? Wish for something to die for?"

"What if I want to watch?" he asked, looking down to unlatch his belt buckle.

She quickly swung her painted baseball bat with grand fashion, repeatedly smashing it against his head. The damage was fatal, and he instantly lay still as a bloody corpse, Calliope standing tall over

LAST FAKE HAPPY WORLD

the murdered monster's body in a frenzy.

No one looked, no one saw.

The bonfire partygoers were lost in their drinking and illegal drugs, making them fit for the massacre that was to come. Skulls were bashed and hearts were broken. Screams were stifled by jaws being bludgeoned, bodies in the middle of random sex acts were positioned dead as one together. The few that fled were lost in the woods and their drug hallucinations, doubling back and falling before the killing Queen. When all was said and done, the bonfire burnt out and thirteen half-naked teenagers lay slaughtered in the woods.

The day's dawn was coming, distant police sirens filling the autumn air. The streets were empty, the monsters were all dead or gone, and Calliope felt release. Her kingdom felt safe again. Soon she was home, soon she was clean from the shower, and soon she packed up her Halloween costume and scepter for another year.

She slept wonderful, much better than she had in a month, with comforting dreams of Kings and Queens, dreams of a kingdom that was safe from attack. Her brain felt alright again, and she awoke with no recollection of any of the prior night's horrors. When she heard the news of the Halloween rampage, she was in just as much shock as everyone else, wondering what sort of monster could do such evil crimes.
Back to life, and back to teaching. Now with an unmistakable feeling of happiness.

LAST FAKE HAPPY WORLD

The following October, Calliope found herself uncontrollably drawn to the Halloween displays and decorations, unusual cravings and off-putting dreams filling her mind at night.

"Ms. Sweetcheck," a young student asked, "what are you doing tomorrow for Halloween?"

Calliope sat at the teacher's desk with a far-away look in her eyes.

"Oh, I'll probably be busy," she answered. "I have a feeling I have a lot of work to do."

The Standoff Opera

The old black van blasted through the mountain roads like a bullet from a rifle. A static-laced AM radio hummed in the background, the trio of news, sports and weather mixed together in a fuzz with the smell of day-old coffee.

"Same garbage," Lester complained, keeping one hand on the wheel and both eyes on the radio dial.

Back to the FM. This was more like it. Reception was always bad in these parts, but familiar songs played on and Lester sang along, his bad singing voice covering the static soundwaves.

He was alone and heading home. It was a road winding through the mountains and the backwoods within - 'Rich Mountain Road.' Not too many cars came this way, a one-way unpaved road winding up and back down the heights. It was an alternate route and practical shortcut, bypassing the tourist traffic and kicking him out relatively near where he needed to be anyways.

The radio fuzzed out completely and he fumbled with the dial. Some sort of foreign channel came in and out. Lester turned the knob completely to the right, and then back to the left. A few channels came through just fine and he settled on a random song, eyes back on the road.

This majestic stretch - He would never forget the first time he saw these mountains. Like anyone, he took so many pictures of the same views, not a single photo capturing the immenseness of it all. Now, spending his life down here, the magic waned just a bit and even somedays was completely lost on him. He almost wished he could see it again with new eyes, to experience it without the everyday dulling effects.

The elevation read nearly 2,000 feet on the van dashboard, then dropping down as low as 1,000 as the vehicle headed downhill. This road was scenic but not something to take lightly. The gravel

LAST FAKE HAPPY WORLD

kicked out beneath tires, fallen branches could block the entire path, and the duration of the road hugged the mountain on one side, the sheer cliff into the forest below on the other. During heavy rain it was impassable, and throughout the winter months the park rangers shut it down completely.

Around a low turn and the elevation began to pick up again. His first time on this road had been a white-knuckle six mph crawl through the six miles of harrowing roadway. 'What if someone's coming the other way?' he had worried back then. A few years later, and not once had a lost tourist or a drunken local been cruising along the wrong direction.

Elevation 1,500 feet and rising. He played with the radio again, something like Italian opera coming through the van's speakers. Not that, anything but that. His finger turned back down the dial, looking for soft rock or something to hold his attention. Elevation at 1,800 feet.

The static got so bad that he turned the radio lower, still exploring his musical options. There, that was it! A familiar and favorite song appeared beneath the static filter. Like a fisherman casting his line, he set to catch the song with precision tuning. The transmission wavered as if shifting. 81.6? No, somewhere else... It was early in the song, but if he took too long, Lester knew he would miss out.

"Come on," he grumbled to himself, his old teeth grinding in his white stubble face. "Come on, baby..."

Elevation was at 2,300 feet now. The unpaved road thrusted rocks out from his tires as he drove with confidence, rounding the blind mountain corners at an increasing speed. The song was nearly halfway finished, he almost had it at channel 81.5 and then lost the reception again.

"Come on!" he yelled at the radio. "It's almost over!"

2,700 feet.

2,800 feet.

The road reached a turn and the song came through, crystal clear

LAST FAKE HAPPY WORLD

for a heavenly minute, his hand still at the dial.
"*Believe me*," the song sang. "*The sun in your eyes, made some of your lies worth beli…*"
The melody cut out to static and Lester pounded at the dashboard. His hand went back to the dial along with his eyes. At 3,000 feet, the mountain pass turned sharply and began its steep drop in elevation.
Lester looked back to the road and slammed the brakes at the sudden turn he had taken dozens of times before. The rocks beneath his tires slid and the van continued moving forward at an unstopping angle.

"Shoot!!" he yelled out, both hands frantically at the wheel, but too late.

The black van skidded to a stop on the edge, the helpless feeling of gravel giving out beneath his tires as the van tipped, falling from the cliffside of the peak elevation.
It plummeted end over end into the forest and foliage far below, hitting the cliffside and tops of trees until at last it crashed and rested. Demolished completely and wholly concealed in the greenery and shadows of the forest.

Absolute black. Lester's eyes were closed, his head pounding with orbital headaches and fear. Was he dead? Paralyzed? All he knew was that he was now on his back in an uncomfortable position. And there were sounds. No, music. The low volume of the van's radio still played, the channel of Italian opera coming through without static.
His arms were flat against cool carbon steel. The inside roof of the van? Somehow, he had survived and been thrown from his seat into the back of the vehicle. He struggled to open his bruised and swollen eyes, seeing nothing and then seeing light. A white light that was too bright and hurt his senses. He closed them in instinct

and squinted as they reopened, closing them again.
But the light was relentless, shining everywhere and brightly through his eyelids, straight into his mind. It was consuming and inescapable, blinding him like staring at the sun and yet somehow absorbing his pain. He forced himself to confront the illumination. His eyes pried opened, staring and focusing into the light and the all-encompassing white.
A shape, there were shapes moving in the pure light like fish underwater. Something drew closer and his battered heart pounded hard. Jaws emerged from the purity, the same milk color of the light but in the shape of a threatening mouth agape.
Lester's hand shook in a fractured ache, but he forced it to his belt and attached holster – There it was, his concealed hand gun – He fingered and pulled at it, the fanged white mouth closing in on him from the light. Its massive canine teeth were just inches from his body.

BANG

With one shot, fate was changed, the white light vanishing from the van as the giant mouth fell. The other shapes retreated, white-gowned angelic shapes that flew from the gunshot like ducks on a pond. They were gone so fast Lester couldn't see them, all fleeing from his sight and traveling like ghosts through the walls of the van.
And in their absence, his pain returned. He had to be imagining such things, the trauma and head injuries of the crash no doubt the cause of such a scene. But as he collected his wits and took deep, hurting breaths, before him lay a physical proof of the strangeness that transpired.

The body of a beautiful woman sat across from Lester in the van. She was colorless in skin, blonde-white hair and a semi-sheer white material robe, all covered in a white bloody substance that

LAST FAKE HAPPY WORLD

poured from the bullet hole in her head. Her eyes expressed pain and she spoke in an alien language, looking at Lester with fear and her arms outreached.

"...Who are you?" he asked to no answer.

She was beautiful, but not just in the ways of a normal woman. There was something that compelled him to feel safe now, at ease despite the tremendous situation. Every thought of the mountain crash temporarily withdrew as he forced himself to try and stand, to try and approach the alluring injured woman.

His leg crunched in agony. No good, the sounds and hurt proved it was heavily fractured or broken. But no matter, for his eyes remained locked on the beauty with the bullet hole in her head, pulling himself slowly across the inside roof-turned-floor of the upside-down van. She was far beyond mesmerizing, her hypnotic and unintelligible voice blending with the barely audible radio opera.

Lester approached, at his bleeding hands and knees to the helpless female that cowered in the corner. He exchanged looks with her, all pain fading for a fleeting moment as he drew inches from her face and her colorless white lips.

"BACK OFF!!" roared a voice that came from below, knocking Lester to his back with his bruised elbows supporting his weight.

All pain returned as he stared at the woman once more, this time below her face and to her shapely body. Beneath her translucent robe and below her breasts, down here there was something more.

"If you come that close again, I will shred your soul with my fangs."

It was the mouth he had seen in the light, the massive jaw that had closed in on him. At the woman's stomach was the white face of a lion, a white mane, eyes and mouth transmutated onto her body.

"What have you done, you pathetic, broken human?"

Lester sat in silence, shaking. He clutched his gun as he studied the creature here before him.

LAST FAKE HAPPY WORLD

"What, what are you??" his uneasy voice asked, blood flavor in his mouth.

He looked to the woman and waited for her answer, but the lion replied in her place.

"We are not at your mercy. You are a mere mortal, we are far outside of your comprehension."

"What were those things that were in here??" Lester asked with a curious fear in his voice. "I'm not crazy, tell me what they were! Some kind of ghosts? What are you?! Tell me or I'll shoot again!"

Sweat cascaded down the neck of the injured Lester. He stared at the lion face beneath the breasts, the strangest thoughts processing through his mind. For all the bewilderment of the accident, and now this, he still couldn't help but feel drawn in toward the woman. He forced himself to resist, at least he had to try.

"It's pointless to use that weapon again, unless you plan to try it on yourself. You've already altered our existence, as well as your own fate, with your reckless decision."

"What do you mean by that?" Lester pointed the gun. "Tell me exactly what you mean."

"Exactly what I mean is exactly what I said," the lion growled.

Lester looked away from the lady with the lion stomach and frantically studied the van's interior. Whatever was going on in here, he needed to escape. But only now he realized just how dire the plummet and crash had been. The van's sides were crushed in, the front seats demolished, and the front doors smashed into oblivion. The rear doors then were the only option for escape in this windowless back of the van. And even in the small chance they still functioned, the woman and her threatening lion stomach were directly beside it in the corner.

"Please," Lester begged in his nervousness, "just tell me what you are, tell me what I did... Am I dead? Did I die here right now??"

The lion watched him with no reaction for a moment, the opera radio song ending and a new one beginning to play. The colorless

LAST FAKE HAPPY WORLD

woman spoke a few words that were lost on Lester's ears, and he caught himself drawn to her again. He resisted.

"Considering this grim state," the white lion pondered out loud, "I'll share with you a simple answer. Do you believe in angels, human?"

Lester continued his gaze and let a chaotic smile break. Small, confused laughs escaped his lips.

"An angel??" he looked her over. "Is that what she's supposed to be? What about the wings? Or the halo?"

The lion's stare penetrated the distance between them, making Lester feel in danger.

"Angel is a human word of a human language," it offered, "a failed attempt to describe what your people can't understand. There are no wings, there is no halo. We travel on planes that you live beside but will never see."

"Tell me what her name is."

"The closest thing that I have to what humans call a 'name' is Nicodemus," he answered.

"Not you, her!" Lester raised his voice, still somewhat entranced by the odd pull of the lady. "I don't care about you, tell me her name."

The woman's face captivated him like no other, and he wondered why he suddenly cared so much. He had seen beautiful women before, mostly on television. But this close, to an 'angel,' if she really was, this was something else and an instantly commanding addiction.

"You truly don't understand what you're dealing with here," Nicodemus explained. "You are but a soul that inhabits soft organs that inhabit hard bones, which in turn are held together by a soft stretching organ. Do you name your skeleton? My 'name' is Nicodemus, and that is the only name we will be known by."

A brief time of no exchanges then passed, the opera nearly forgotten in the background, the same as Lester's horrible injuries from the crash. This was past the limits of known reality. Trapped

LAST FAKE HAPPY WORLD

in the wreckage of his van, a standoff with a talking lion's head in the body of an angel. He held his handgun still, the sole feeling of safety.

"So, am I dead then?" Lester asked. "If she – if *you* are what you say you are, then I'm already dead, aren't I?"

The lion remained silent, its predator eyes locked on the injured man like a wounded dinner.

"Just answer me!" Lester screamed, the violent shout hurting his lungs inside. "Tell me why you're here! Tell me or take me to Heaven!"

"Is that how it works?" Nicodemus laughed. "Heaven or Hell?"

In his broken body, Lester inched towards the angel again and the lion roared, its gaping jaw stretching abnormally to show rows of deadly teeth.

"Make no mistake," it said as Lester stayed back, "I am what I say I am, I was here to take your soul away."

"Then do it! Show me!"

"Still, you bark your pathetic demands at me? Do you realize that the minute you crashed, you were to die? We came here to claim your soul. When I materialized to take you, when I became what is physical in your realm to release your soul into mine, you forfeited everything. Now I lay here with my holy host, bleeding Heaven's blood for your sin."

The preaching anger in Nicodemus' voice struck a message into Lester that stuck. He looked at the divine being with a hindered awe, what had he done? If this was death, if this was a messenger of God to carry him into the afterlife, what now then?

"There were others," Lester reminded himself out loud. "If you can't take me now, they'll come back, won't they? They can take my soul, there were more angels."

"Human, what don't you understand? Do you really believe that your tiny existence in this infinity is that important? Do you truly believe that they'll send more angels for you to try and kill?"

"I didn't mean to do it! I was scared, I didn't know -"

LAST FAKE HAPPY WORLD

"What's done is done, I was sent for you and your soul was mine to reap. Now here we sit, pathetic creatures to die a pathetic death, nothing more."

Lester shook the feeling, he might have screwed this up, but he wasn't giving up on life, even at this brink of death.

"But if my soul's not yet taken," he asked, "can I still live? If I can get out, and get help, I can keep living, right?"

The lion-angel seemed annoyed at the question.

"You can do what you want, I have no power anymore to harvest your soul. Who can say what that means for you? Maybe you'll finish dying, or maybe you'll live forever in that broken, mangled body. Or maybe you'll even be one of the souls that wander your world for eternity. Do what you will, if you can manage to escape this created prison."

Lester visually searched the ruins of his van, upside-down and compacted. There had to be a way, his sight constantly returning to the rear doors.

"However," the lion added, "as you've prematurely brought my existence to its fate, you must serve me in this request."

Lester didn't reply, not wanting to agree and still focused on the doors.

"Feed me," the lion ordered. "I will die a physical death just the same as you, but my bond with this host body demands I survive as long as I can."

"There's no food in here," Lester informed it, slowly pulling himself toward the rear doors.

He was so near them already, yet so near the open mouth of the lion as well. With caution he kept his distance, alert and fearful for whatever remained of his life.

"I'm not feeding you me," Lester professed, "if that's what you were thinking."

"Though my intent was to take your soul, I would sooner die than live off of your poisoned flesh," Nicodemus snarled. "But for every moment I spend in this physical state, I am slowly expiring.

LAST FAKE HAPPY WORLD

My request is that you feed me from the *Vault of Heaven*."

"Even if I knew what you meant -"

"DO IT!!"

The lion roared, hot saliva spitting onto the skin of Lester. He turned to the angel's humanoid face, the white blood crusted around the bullet hole in her head.

"Feed me what lies inside," Nicodemus grumbled. "You may leave this intended grave of your would-be death but heed my final demand."

Lester looked into the eyes of the beautiful face, the angel's mouth still saying the soft words that his mind couldn't grasp.

"You want me to feed you what's 'inside' of her??"

"It's not unlike the brain that exists in your human skull. Feed it to me, so that I may exist with my host one moment more in eternity."

"What if I just let you die?"

"Don't invoke my wrath… My physical manifestation can still destroy your fragile human form."

Lester turned his head back and forth from the angel's face to the lion's mouth, to the van's rear doors and back again. This demand was too much, he needed to flee and move quickly, leaving this injured creature and nightmare far behind.

A small burst of movement and Lester tried for the doors, pitifully reaching them as the lion growled within jaw-range. Inverted and dented, the old doors moved a small bit but not by much. He pushed and pulled with all of his might, Nicodemus beginning to snarl.

"I could feed on you right now," the creature bragged. "We would both die with you impaled on my teeth, but it would be a fitting end to this unanticipated comedy."

"What do you want me to do??" Lester complained as he rocked the bent doors back and forth.

"Feed me from the Vault of Heaven, as I already have instructed you. Do as I say, and you can continue prying these doors to your heart's content."

"... Just to be clear, you want me to feed you her brain, and you won't eat me? You'll leave me alone to work on these doors?"

He gave it another unsuccessful tug before the lion even answered. It wasn't moving much, but judging by the complete destruction of the van's front end, this was more than likely his only way out.

"Correct. Perform the act now, or else I'll make sure we both meet our end accordingly."

Lester ran ideas through his mind. There weren't many options left to consider. He knew that he had two bullets left in his gun, but shooting the angel again wasn't realistic. If these doors never opened, he would need those bullets for suicide. The first to shoot himself, the second if the first shot failed.

"Fine, I'll do it," he gave in, kneeling before the injured angel. "How in the world do I even..."

He raised his hands before the angel's head, the handgun back in its holster. Nervously looking down to her lion stomach, so near to its jaws, he tried to trust it and returned his gaze to her face. An angel. This close, both breathing their dying breath on each other, she was intoxicating to his mind. It wasn't natural, and Lester recognized that. But the attraction to her alluring beauty was out of this world and he struggled to resist it.

"Do what I've instructed you to do," Nicodemus reminded him. "No man should be allowed this close to the body of an angel, appreciate it if you must, but do nothing more than what I ordered you to do."

Alert of the dangerous mouth below, he looked into the heavenly woman's eyes. She said her words, indecipherable yet somehow more musical than the opera music playing. She was too perfect, and he lingered, his hand nearly going for her cheek before the lion growled and interrupted.

"Do it now! Stop hesitating!!"

Lester regained focus, his hands moving from her cheek and then rising to the temple of her head, to the spot where the entrance wound of the bullet still showed.

"I don't know how you expect me to even get -" he said and then stopped.

Where his fingers touched her forehead, it gave way. It pushed in like soft clay, crumbling indentations where he pressed. Her words remained, something like tears in her eyes even though she didn't cry.

Lester cringed, his fingers going into her head and touching a gelatin rather than skull. White blood oozed onto his hand, the skin below her hairline caving in like piecrust, her reaction relatively unphased.

"Excellent, human," Nicodemus applauded. "Deliver the fruit and I will allow you to continue."

Lester felt an uneasy turn in his stomach as he gingerly gripped at something unseen. It felt like a peeled egg in his grasp, leaning back as he pulled it forward, out from the brittle skin of her forehead.

It was brilliant, a glowing gold shape that moved like living fat in his cupped fingers. The sight of it was magical yet repulsive at once, elements of an angel's brain sitting there in the palm of his hand.

"Feed it to me!"

Lester fumbled it in his grip and then lowered it to the lion's mouth. He didn't dare set it in and instead let it slide off, the small golden mass landing on the beast's tongue, its mouth then closing. Lester watched for an instant as it chewed, then remembered the task at hand.

With no idea of how long he had before the lion turned on him, he set to working on the doors, the angel's female voice still muttering unusual words. He struggled, rocking them back and forth. Small results were coming, the crushed double door making small movements as if it were possibly wedging free.

"Ohhh..." the lion sighed in ecstasy. "So sensational..."

LAST FAKE HAPPY WORLD

Lester paid it no mind, nervously tugging at the doors with what small strength he had. Any moment the lion could bite at him, the angel's body so close to the only way out.

"You know, I imagined that it would taste indescribable," it continued post-meal, "but this was even beyond my own lofty expectations. If I could function my host's arms well enough, I would be fit to serve myself... However, as it stands..."

"What?" Lester asked as he continued trying to unjam the doors. "You want more? Is there even anymore in there?"

"You said you would feed me if I allowed you to continue."

"I thought you meant one time!"

Lester took no chances at being devoured and turned sideways to remove more of the angel's brain. Again, just as before, he hesitated. Even with the top of her soft head pushed in, she was still inhumanly captivating. The blood milk dripped down her face and slender body like wet sugar, Lester's fingers scooping out another small handful of the golden brain.

"Here," he told Nicodemus, dropping it to the waiting tongue. "Try to make it last this time!"

He returned to his door work, his fingers covered in the angel blood. Why was she still so beautiful, even in this un-angelic state? He looked over at her again from the doors. Aside from the chewing lion, her body was so perfect. For whatever reason, he found himself in increasing states of desire.

"Not now..." he mumbled to himself. "Not... now..."

"I can smell your pheromones," Nicodemus told him, licking its lips. "I can read your scent. Don't let your temptation guide you."

"I won't, I just need to get this damn door open."

"The fruit is so enticing," the lion continued. "I think I need more of it, human..."

"Already?? Come on!"

"I will devour you like the tempted snake you are!" Nicodemus yelled, the hot breath from deep within making Lester's bruised skin sweat.

LAST FAKE HAPPY WORLD

"Ok, ok! Relax! Give me a second!"

He turned and reached into the angel's head again, this time mesmerized by her face for longer than before. The attraction was at its summit, her crumbling face and white blood dripping like candle wax on an immaculate body. The lion roared, but Lester couldn't break the trance. This temptation was far past the reach of a man's sexual control.

With each look, the pull had been stronger. With every touch inside her head, a more intimate connection. This was no earthly woman. This was an angel, the ultimate perfection of design. Her effect was never to be felt by a mere man, but now it was past the point of return. Thoughts of escape were depleted, replaced by an irrepressible lust that became uncontrollably natural.

The draw was impossible to break, the lion roaring menacing threats.

"She belongs to me, not you! This forbidden fruit belongs to me!"

But the words came from the human Lester, not Nicodemus. He forced himself against her, his quivering lips on her crumbling face, his broken hands around her heavenly body.

For a brief, impossibly short moment, she was his. Human flesh against Heaven's flesh, materialized. No man would ever know the pleasure he felt just in her warmth, no human woman could ever offer a man what she was able to radiate without effort.

The lion Nicodemus roared and attacked, biting and eating, teeth clamping down on the already half-dead Lester. The size of the man was too much in his physical form, the angel's lion stomach coughing and struggling, choking on his shape and gagging until neither dying creature moved at all anymore. Lester's legs dangled from the lion's mouth. The angel's beautiful and shattered face stopped speaking, the remainder of her golden brain draining out.

And there, buried forever in a van within the trees and foliage of

LAST FAKE HAPPY WORLD

the mountain drop, the secret struggle between Earth and Heaven came to a sudden and sadistic finale. The Italian opera continued to play from the radio, lingering over the scene for a while more, eventually coming to an end as the van's battery died out.

A broken man graced by an angel, and a perfect angel, ruined by an everyday man.

LAST FAKE HAPPY WORLD

Familiar Faces

The ongoing rains of April had brought pockets of street flooding across the low-lying streets of Wirkine. This was tremendous to the city's children, the school district closed and so then a spontaneous 'second spring break' was happening.
Eleven-year-old Luna sat alongside her eight-year-old brother Simon, watching reruns of old cartoons a few feet away from the television. Their father sat distracted, reading last week's Sunday paper again, the last that was delivered before the heavy rain.
"Honey!" their mother called to the room of the distracted three. "They're sitting too close to the TV again. They're ruining their eyes."
"Kids," their dad said with hardly a glance over the paper, "back on the couch. Both of you."
Luna turned, her freckled face looking back beneath her curly black hair, Simon still watching unphased.
"Hey!" their mother stood in the frame of the hallway. "Away from that television, you two!"
Luna tugged on her brother's shirt, only slightly breaking his daze, and led him to their old worn out couch.
"You have to keep a better eye on them."
"Gotcha," their father replied, his nose still buried in the news, eyes half closed.

The cartoons carried on throughout the morning, fun violence and wild adventures, an escape from their week-long holdings in the house. By afternoon, the Sliwinski family sat around the table and ate lunch together, the refrigerator and cabinets slowly thinning out over this extended stay at home.
"I'll call the office again, later today," Dad mentioned. "The streets should be clearing out in a day or two. I'll have so much crap to do once -"

LAST FAKE HAPPY WORLD

"Language?" his wife stopped him, Simon giggling as Luna just looked at him. "Not around the children!"

"Right... Stuff, I have so much *stuff* that I need to take care of."

"Well, I'm running out of things to make a decent meal with," Mom admitted. "As soon as that street clears up, we're all going down to the grocery store to fill this house up with good food again."

"I don't want good food," Simon complained, twirling a fork at his unappealing leftovers.

"Well, that's too bad," Mom carried on. "You can't always have everything that you want."

"I don't know about you guys," Dad announced, standing up and heading to the counter, "but what I think we need right about now is a couple of cookies."

Simon and Luna cheered him on as their mom put her hands to her head. "You are so incorrigible."

Dad helped himself and the kids to a few chocolate chip cookies, giving a thumbs-up to his disapproving wife.

"All of you are ridiculous, absolutely ridiculous."

As she cleared their plates off from the table and briefly stood by the sink, her eyes set through the window at the flooded street outside.

"Honey?" she asked her husband. "It's not going to rain at all today, is it?"

"Not that I'm aware of," he replied, the sound of cookie crumbs in his voice. "There's nothing in the forecast for the rest of the week, thank goodness."

"How do you think Mrs. Penrich is holding up? That poor old lady's all by herself over there, maybe we should stop in?"

"No, no. She's fine. She's a tough old broad. Besides, she's got that goofy son of hers to check up on her."

"The goofy son that never visits? Say, Luna," Mrs. Sliwinski turned and called out to her daughter, both kids back on the couch already.

LAST FAKE HAPPY WORLD

"Why don't you and your brother go next door and check on Mrs. Penrich? I'm sure she would love to see you."

"Mom, do we have to??" Luna protested. "Why don't you guys go?"

"You kids have been cooped up in this house all week, watching television like a bunch of couch potatoes. Some fresh air will do you good!"

Simon's eyes narrowed under his short brown hair, looking to their father for help. "I don't want to go, I don't like her."

"Simon," his mother addressed him, "that's not polite to say. She's a bit eccentric, but she's a sweet old lady. You two are going to go next door and check on her, understood? I'm sure it would mean the world to her to see your smiling faces."

Both children looked to their father, who kept his lips sealed, silently hoping that he wouldn't have to go next door as well.

"Come on already, Simon," Luna called back to her little brother, crossing the soggy grass of the swampy front yard.

It was a strange day outside, not a car in the stagnant river of a street, the sky full of stormy swirls of cloud. Every step they made squished down in the water-logged soil, entertaining Simon to no end. Finally, Luna went to take him by the arm, coaxing him on to the house next door.

Mrs. Penrich's house sat before them, so nondescript. If someone had quizzed Luna about the color, the shape, or even how many windows, she would have gotten it all wrong. It was a constant presence every day, but somehow so dull and dismissible. They would see the old lady from time to time, getting the mail or raking the leaves, but those were the only occasions. It felt quite unusual now walking toward the structure, but here they were, standing on the doorstep of the old lady next door.

Luna held a small care package from her mother, Simon standing directly behind her and peeking around her side.

"Don't be weird," she ordered, getting up the courage to ring the half painted-over doorbell.

"I want to go back home..."

Just as Luna turned to tell her brother otherwise, the white door of the vanilla house creaked open. Both children turned their eyes to the world within, old Mrs. Penrich standing there in wait.

"Umm," Luna stumbled through her thoughts, holding up the bag in offering. "We live next door, and um, our mom wanted us to bring you this…"

Mrs. Penrich looked Luna over first, followed by what little she could see of Simon behind his sister. The old lady was quite a sight with a floral print nightgown and slippers, oversized glasses and unkempt short white hair. A facial mole and whisker stood out like a magnet for the children's eyes, Luna trying not to stare.

"The Sliwinski children, I know you two," she grumbled, a strange smoker's voice through her denture teeth. "Come in, come in, let's have a look at what your mother sent you with."

Luna looked to Simon, who didn't take his eyes off his big sister, and both slowly stepped through the open doorway, leading like a portal into the unknown next-door home. A glance back at her family's house, and Luna held her breath, nervously walking in.

The odd interior of the Penrich household lay before them. Immediately in the front room, the walls were crowded with shelves and display cabinets, collectables of all varieties visible in a sensory overload. Both children's greedy eyes pulled in the scenery, Mrs. Penrich standing aside as they basked in its glory.

Floor to ceiling, old and new statues of movie heroes and villains, black and white movie posters, framed and displayed down a hallway. A set of shelves that held odd trinkets and small stuffed animals, one of every variety imaginable in the wealth of this collection.

"I don't get too many visitors anymore," she said, allowing them to be mesmerized by the collective excess. "Please, have a look. I have trouble throwing things away."

And continue looking they did. Simon no longer hid behind his sister, venturing out on the shaggy mustard-color carpet to the shelves, gawking with the same wide eyes he had at the television earlier. The collection of offbeat memorabilia was meticulously placed and set in the display style of a do-it-yourself museum. Dolls of showgirls and figures of classic horror, posed side by side like a contrast of good and evil. Luna looked too, Mrs. Penrich relieving her of the care package and taking it to what was presumed to be the kitchen.

"Don't try to touch anything," Luna instructed her brother, the strangeness of this all not lost on her young mind. "These aren't toys."

"Does the boy like toys?" the returning old lady asked. "What is your first name, young man?"

He paused, looking back from the arranged knick-knacks and to the woman, saying nothing.

"His name is Simon," Luna told her, annoyed by her shy brother's constant spaciness.

"Simon," Mrs. Penrich repeated in her rumbly voice. "A fine name for such a strong looking boy. Like the brave *Simon de Montfort*."

She exchanged a look with Luna, who knew nothing of the name just said, and then returned her attention back to the young boy.

"I have history books and old paintings on those old-world subjects, boring hobbies to you children, I know. But Simon, how would you like to see my life's collection of rare and unusual toys?"

His face lit up at the neighbor's suggestion, the thrill of toys overtaking his fear and resistance.

"We should probably get back home," Luna made an attempt to step between them.

"No!" Simon exclaimed. "I want to see the toys!"

LAST FAKE HAPPY WORLD

Mrs. Penrich laughed at the reaction. "Very well, as long as your sister says that it's fine."

Caught in the middle of the elderly look and joyful eyes, Luna had no choice but to agree. "Ok, but we'll go home after that. Mom and Dad will be waiting for us."

Mrs. Penrich nodded approvingly. "Please sit down, dear," she motioned Luna to the reupholstered couch, leading Simon away as she took him by the hand. "I'll be right back."

Luna watched and finally gave in to the good feeling, watching her brother walk up the stairs with their elderly neighbor. Their grandparents had passed away before they were alive, and though this was no replacement, it eased her heart to watch the scene.

Sitting there alone for that moment, Luna couldn't help but look around at the unordinary number of things surrounding her. Who collected this much stuff? Her parents had some clutter, but it was nothing like this. For a nondescript house, this was too much to describe, she saw as much as she could at once. An overall sense of uneasiness took over. Why did it feel like everything was watching her? Every statue, every framed poster and collectable had a face or many faces, all looking blindly out and staring at her. Her imagination ran wild, the manic trance broken only by the returning Mrs. Penrich.

"He's such a doll," she said as she slowly helped herself down the stairway, returning alone now. "I wish you children would have stopped over sooner. How is your family faring with the flood?"

Luna waited, allowing the lady to complete her descent on the stairs, slowly walking over and then eventually joining her on the couch.

"Good, I suppose..."

"You mean *well*, child," Mrs. Penrich corrected her. "One does well, not *good*."

Luna sat still, sitting up straight and nervous about everything from grammar to posture. "Is my brother alright up there, all by himself?"

LAST FAKE HAPPY WORLD

"Why wouldn't he be? There are so many things for him to see, things that will inspire his imagination. Mementos. You never did tell me your first name, Ms. Sliwinski."

"Luna, Ma'am," she replied, trying to remain as courteous as possible.

"Luna..." Mrs. Penrich said and let the name linger, letting it sit for an uncomfortable moment on her tongue. "What a glorious name. A young girl, like a crescent moon building toward full maturity. Your parents have quite the knack for naming children! Did you know that there is a face on the moon? The 'man on the moon' was what we used to call it when I was young."

Luna didn't reply, unsure of what to say as Mrs. Penrich continued without pause.

"Then again, I see faces in everything. A bit of a pareidoliac, I've been told. You know, everyone has some sort of face-recognition waves in their brain. We can recognize patterns and facial features in things. But some people, such as myself, see more faces than others. Do you see faces, Luna?"

Luna sat confused, this random information filtering through her impressionable mind. The eyes of the vast collection felt even more focused on her now and she shifted in her seat, feeling uneasy once again.

"Be calm, Luna," Mrs. Penrich instantly noticed and eased her, her blue-veined pale hand coming down onto Luna's leg.

"May, may I use your bathroom, please?" the young girl jumped up in disarray, saying the first thing she could think to say. "It's an emergency."

"Oh, my! Of course," the frail lady replied, sitting at the couch. "Through the kitchen, dear. First door in the hallway."

"Thank you!" Luna replied fast and walked briskly across the room, eyes looking forward and at nothing.

Once she passed into the kitchen, then around the corner where her neighbor couldn't see her, she paused and let her posture down, heart racing hard with a souring taste in her stomach. Luna wasn't

LAST FAKE HAPPY WORLD

completely sure why she felt so uncomfortable, but something wasn't right.

And this kitchen... Even in here, so many things she couldn't believe. Walls covered in calendars of years past, art and photos of people with beautiful faces. High above, around all edges of the room, a wall mounted shelf with character art on salt and pepper shakers, china and decoration plates. The refrigerator was covered with magnets of famous old musicians and celebrities, and then centered atop a small dining table, a framed photograph of who Luna assumed to be Mr. and Mrs. Penrich. In front of this same nondescript house, Mr. Penrich looked feeble and thin, an oddball in an ill-fitting suit next to his beautiful wife.

Luna took a quick, closer look, the striking woman in a fancy dress and blouse, as beautiful as a movie star. Was that really the same old lady that lived here, the same withered soul that had just sat so uncomfortably close to her on the couch? It had to be, many years ago.

Her peripheral vision pulled her sight away, toward the garbage canister and what was that? Atop the waste sat her mother's care package, sitting there in the trash, thrown out without a care.

There was an electric-zap sound in the air, from outside or another room, a daytime flash of the lights on and off, then the sound of the refrigerator going silent. A power outage?

"Oh dear, not again," Mrs. Penrich complained from the living room, the sound of steps then as she headed toward the kitchen.

Luna thought about her brother and freaked out, rushing back to the living room, brushing past her elderly neighbor.

"Don't worry, sweetheart, it happens all the time."

But Luna paid her no mind, dashing up the stairs she had last seen Simon go. Downstairs, the outside light illuminated the dark house well enough, but up here the clutter was cloaked in sheer nothingness, Luna calling for her brother and feeling for a hallway door.

"Simon!" she yelled, pressing on walls and no response, her eyes adapting quickly to the shadowy change. "Simon, let's go! Where are you?"

His lack of response was nothing unusual, but it struck her with panic to no end.

"Simon, I'm not playing around! We're going home now!"

"Luna," the rough voice of Mrs. Penrich called from the stairway, "is something wrong? What are you fussing about up there?"

Luna spied a doorway in the darkened hall and walked in, her eyes picking out more collectables and organized mess, feeling for structure and inadvertently knocking something from a shelf. It crashed to a carpet-less floor, the sound of shattering porcelain filling the silent home.

"What in the Lord's name are you doing up there, child?? Do be careful!"

Luna continued her rush and left the room, advancing through the shadowy hall and then through the next doorway – Simon!

It was difficult to see, but Luna could see her brother huddled in the corner, alone in the dark and scared, clutching at something in his tiny arms.

"Simon, I was calling you! Come on! Let's go!"

He looked at her, frozen in fear, until she came and grabbed at him, pulling him to his feet.

"What are you holding?"

"It's a stuffed animal, I was scared..."

Luna pulled the toy from his small shaking hands and went to set it on the floor. For a moment she paused, feeling the off-putting texture and solidity of it. It reminded her of something she had learned about last year.

"This isn't a stuffed animal, Simon!" she told him, putting it down fast. "Remember that store on vacation?? The one that sold the dead animals??"

"Taxidermy, it's called," came the voice of the old lady, either on the staircase or in the hallway. "Such beautiful faces, animals have."

LAST FAKE HAPPY WORLD

Luna pulled her brother roughly, not letting him have a say in what they did next. As she led from the room, she could see some of the other 'toys' he had been surrounded by, everything from animal skulls to full skeletons and taxidermy oddities. They fled into the hallway, Luna disoriented in direction, no light to lead her way.

The children headed one way then turned back and went the other. Which way was it now? They passed an open-door room and Simon briefly pulled free of Luna's grip, looking in and almost entering.

Adult pictures were taped to the walls and fornicating figurines were held in the shadows, a collection unfit for their innocent eyes. Luna rushed Simon away, back into the hallway.

A bounding glow of candle light began to grow on a distant wall, Luna in her fear pulling the opposite direction. Mrs. Penrich had gone from the peculiar next-door neighbor to someone much more foreboding in the span of the last twenty minutes. Surely by now their parents would be headed over, Luna hoped, wondering what their children were doing. Nothing was wrong, yet somehow everything was wrong. The candle light grew brighter.

Luna ducked into a room, pulling Simon along. How large was this house, anyway? The room was different than the others, more spacious and littered with unseen things that felt like paper. The sound of Mrs. Penrich's feet shuffled near, the light coming closer to the room's door, and then it stopped.

"God awful children," she muttered, approaching in the hallway, her voice a grainier rumble now. "Come into my house and rummage through my life, without a care or even a single ounce of God damned respect."

The tone in her voice was terrifying, transmogrifying from the kind hearted old lady and into something far past their youthful understanding.

"Blasphemous offspring... Who asked you to come here? The child-witch named Luna, let me see that porcelain face... Did you know that the famous Simon de Montfort is burning in Hell for his sins? He seduced his sister; his body was ripped to pieces on the battlefield!"

Luna covered her brother's ears as he began to bawl, neither understanding what she was screaming about, but recognizing the warped anger in her tone.

Simon shook harder as the candle light grew, illuminating the room and its now-seen hoarded collection of black and white photographs. Luna looked back to keep hold of her brother and then she saw it. Behind them, propped upright in a rocking chair, sat the decayed remains of a human body, dressed in the same fancy dress and blouse that Mrs. Penrich had worn in that old kitchen photograph.

The shock of the body propelled Luna and Simon away, but faced before them on the opposing side was a living sight worse than death.

Mrs. Penrich stood before them without her nightgown on, her nudity in full display. Her shriveled and elderly body revealed in that single horrifying moment that she was not at all who she had claimed to be.

The real Mrs. Penrich was dead, sitting here in the cobwebbed rocking chair and rotting. Mr. Penrich had taken her identity and had been living in her guise, alone in this mess.

Luna screamed and Simon too, rushing past the naked elderly man and his revolting spider-veined flesh, knocking the candle from his grip as he reached wildly to grab the two.

They raced past and he shouted in an odd voice between man and woman. "Bastards! No!!"

But he didn't pursue as they fled, his obsession was with the collection, the faces he couldn't throw out. The fallen candle lit the photographs of the strangers he had amassed, their unknown yet familiar faces burning like a massacre. Tears roared down his aged face as the flames rolled sweat down his exposed body.

From room to room the fire spread as the children ran to escape.

LAST FAKE HAPPY WORLD

The room of people's photos and the body of his wife. The room of taxidermy animals now aflame. Every room of the entire house, every collected object that had a face, or something that looked like a face, set on fire and Mr. Penrich screamed as he lost it all at once. A living Hell in his confused Heaven, a lifetime of obsession burning up in the undiscerning blaze.

The fire engines came, driving through the flooded streets and making miniature waves as the entire block gathered outside. Simon and Luna trembled beneath a blanket, held closely by their loving parents, watching the house of collected horror completely engulfed in the inferno. As the fire fighters tried to contain it, Luna looked to the house shape and swore she saw a face. The smoky upstairs windows were like eyes, the open doorway like a mouth.

But there was something more, and Luna gasped.

From the black smoke of the burning house, another face.

It writhed and twisted in the smog, the tormented face of Mr. Penrich's soul, disintegrating into the sky before the rising moon.

The Curse of Hexcera

Black lightning crashed from the far heavens above, striking the forest beyond the accursed castle. The rumble of its impact echoed through the land.

"What brings you down into my kingdom, barbarian? I have not summoned you or any other witless dog to my realm."

"A village at the end of your land's reach. I only visit by their payment to me."

The lady laughed, a witch's cackle from her deceptively young appearance. Her hair was as dark as night, as long as its endless hours. It poured down her upper body, partially concealing her displayed upper half.

"And how much gold is my death worth to them?" she asked, gathering a furred black cloak around her naked sides.

"I'll receive payment after I end this night."

The witch Hexcera got up from her bone ribcage throne and approached the barbarian. His heavy muscle tightened as he gripped ready at the broadsword.

"Easy," she calmed him, setting her hand at the sword. "I am not the cause of this never-ending night. You've simply fallen for the hysterics of those common people."

The distance was closed between them, Hexcera standing face to face with Kalanog the barbarian, her hands on his toned chest.

"Why do you wear this mask?" she questioned him, touching at his black half-skull helmet. "Show me your true face."

Kalanog pressed the witch off, returning to his senses.

"I will show you my true face when you show me yours," he bartered, the lady stepping back to the throne and returning to her seat.

A small window of silence passed in this spoken game. Hexcera looked Kalanog over. His rippled muscle ridden with old scars, that face-concealing black skull helmet with wild, unwashed black and silver hair. His leather skin shown, black fur boots and a black fur loincloth. Only a heavy broadsword in his hand and a battle axe strapped to his back.

"You aren't well enough prepared for what evil faces you."

"I've slayed a hundred witches and a thousand demons stronger than you could ever be."

Hexcera sighed, slumping in her throne. "Do you even know what you are dealing with? Tell me, how was your journey to my castle? How was the forest?"

"I stayed on the path, there was no danger."

"No danger, you dare say?" she burst out in surprise, shocked by his impudence. "Then you must have a penchant for strange luck, most men would die even with staying on the path. Tell me now what you intend to do, now that you have gotten through to me."

With the sword gripped and held ready, Kalanog spoke. "I demand that you remove your wicked spell of night, by words or by force."

Hexcera seemed eased, or at least amused by the man's tenacity.

"If I were to remove the single spell I've cast, all that would happen is that this castle would fall, and I, along with you now here, would perish with it. The night would still remain."

"Remove it now and we will see."

"Your brain doesn't quite understand, barbarian," she drilled into him. "My spell shields this castle, holds it up against the intruders. As I've said, I am not the cause of this relentless night."

Kalanog stood without emotion, Hexcera waiting and then continuing her words.

"If you truly want to end this curse, if you think that you're strong enough to end it, you will work for me instead of that village. Do what I ask, and my payment will stretch beyond anything they could ever dream of offering you."

She crossed her long legs in the throne of bones and held the barbarian's attention.

"Kill everything in this forest," she instructed him. "Do you love death? The forest that surrounds my castle is infested with every devil, demon and wicked creature this world has ever seen. When they came, they brought this relentless night along with them. Feed your lust for destruction. Slay them, slay every demon in these woods until you see the sun come up again, and then you will have your reward of me, barbarian."

Hexcera and Kalanog locked eyes with one another. His lust of destruction was only met by his lust of carnal flesh, the fire that was raging in his eyes seething through the eye-holes of the skull helmet. The blood of demons would rain down tonight from the thunderous swing of his mighty blade - and then - drunk from the drowning flood of their extinction, he would claim his prize of flesh.

The descending, winding pathway from Hexcera's castle was the passageway to a trail of doom. Every sound was the cry of war, every shadow movement a stalking death.

Kalanog left the path as soon as it leveled out, entering the trees and overgrowth of the foreboding forest. Broadsword at the ready, muscles rearing to react, and his eyes captured every small light in the darkness.

Another crash of black lightning in the woods, the thunderous boom startling something in the brush. Kalanog stopped and gave wait. Goblin creatures emerged with hooked sticks and makeshift shields, stabbing at Kalanog like a rabid pack of hyenas.

He dodged and felt only the smallest stab at the skin of his arm, answering back with death-dealing strikes and a spinning flail of decapitation. The miniscule heads of the foolhardy goblins fell to the ground in short work. If this was the level of evil that the forest held, he would be in Hexcera's bedchamber with ease, the sun shining in these woods again.

A sound from the trees to his right alerted him, slithering vines reaching and wrapping around his legs, tightening and small thorns puncturing his thick skin. A swing of the sword and they fell, noxious fumes hissing in emergence from the slashes. More vines lashed out, this time grabbing at his arms as well as his legs. With brute force he muscled through, unable to swing his blade but hanging on, pulled forward by the overwhelming plant life. This was only a minor struggle, choosing to conserve his strength when it met with no avail. Dragged onward, helpless and bound, through the evil forest and Kalanog prepared himself for the opening.

In a grove of twisted trees, the vines pulled him forward and up, lifting him to feed to the gaping mouth of a mutated carnivorous plant. With a burning splash, it released and plummeted him into the digestive acid within, the dissolving bones of eaten creatures disintegrating beside him.

In a thick cut, Kalanog tore through the enclosure of the gorging plant, tipping its contents and spilling the acidic juice out and to the ground. The dripping pool burned at his skin to no reaction, and with downward stabs he slit the remains of the wild vines, stepping over them and through the air's pollen, continuing deeper and into the dark.

There were bear-wolves and giants, demon birds and man-sized spiders. Alternating between his broadsword and the battle axe, Kalanog spilled the intestines and crushed the skulls of all that opposed him. Leaving no life alive in his wake, he plowed through orcs and manticores, slaying giant toads and hives of dog-sized insects. Trolls and armored boars fell to him. Mutant scorpions and dragon worms, screaming harpies and reanimated skeletons. Kalanog battled without exhaustion, screams and death cries filling the immortal night as he severed appendages from the enemy hordes. Bathed in blood, he fought on, bit by broken fangs and cut by infected claws.

This was becoming a night unlike any other, a power struggle he had not anticipated, but now fully embraced. War. Destruction. Death after violent death. Black lightning crashed all around him.

LAST FAKE HAPPY WORLD

Pools of slime latched onto his boots, only to be stomped into oblivion. Nests were found, eggs were trampled. There was a giraffe-necked creature like a hydra, jaws chomping and then every throat slit. Demon after demon, abominations of monstrosities and terror, all cut down and pulverized into mountains of bloody meat.

The eternal midnight went on, the unworldly screams of horror filling the air in a chorus of misery. Blood and bile, broken bones and piles of tentacles and teeth. Bogs of shambling mudmen and skies filled with bats made of fire, nothing surprised him anymore. Every beast that attacked was met and destroyed, every demon that fled was hunted down and slaughtered. Blood flooded the ground, fur and flesh flying into the sky. The killing orgy continued into the everlasting night.

Shadow-illuminated by a dark flash of lightning, Kalanog came face to face with a serpentine terror in the forest. Coiled as tall as the trees it haunted, the gargantuan snake hissed with a forked tongue, its eyes watching the barbarian as if he were a defenseless rat. Kalanog assumed a battle stance, his axe at the ready.

The demonic monster snake struck, faster than the constant lightning and without fear, meeting the battle-weary Kalanog in midair. The poisonous fangs of the scaled monster met the blood-drenched axe of the warrior…

Hexcera stood in a candlelit bedroom chamber, brushing her hair when the barbarian Kalanog burst in. His body reeked of death, dried blood and wet slime stamped across his flesh.

"The quest is as complete as it will ever be," he then declared, dropping the severed-end of the giant snake's tongue at the floor. "I'm here to claim my reward."

"Finished already?" Hexcera looked to him. "I figured you were here to rest and try again tomorrow."

LAST FAKE HAPPY WORLD

"There will never be a tomorrow for you, witch," Kalanog told her. "I confronted every dark corner of your forest. I destroyed everything that breathed or moved -"

"Then why is the sun not back?" she mockingly interrupted.

"For the same reason that I still hear the bear-wolves howl," he continued in anger. "The sun never rose, but I was out there for two cycles of a day. For every giant I killed, two more stood tall. For every egg I smashed, another demon was born. I traveled back the path I walked, and every single thing I slayed was alive again twofold."

Even as he talked, the massive snake tongue on the floor began to squirm.

"See that, witch? Do you believe me to be blind??"

"Calm yourself. It is indeed a vexing curse on this land, but you've only just begun to understand it. You need to rest," she comforted him and touched his helmet. "You need to rest your body and mind and continue for me."

As Hexcera spoke, she bewitched him, looking deeply into his mind until he cast his sword aside. She walked backwards, leading him toward the foot of her bed with a mix of lust and magic. The blood-stained barbarian loomed over her, and all thoughts were briefly forgotten, the beautiful dark-haired witch so enticing here before him.

"Have an early taste of your reward, barbarian," she coaxed him, waiting for his strong embrace.

By the light of the castle's candles he went to her, only halfway in control. Her figure lay bare atop the black fur cloak, her hand motioning for him to join her.

And he gave in. He leaned into her body and felt his scars against her soft flesh. Her nails, like claws, dug into his soiled skin as he kissed and held her closely. Hexcera pulled at her cloak and then wrapped it around herself and her lover, like a blanket as they continued the initial moments of their brutal passion.

But something awoke in his entranced mind. The cloak around

LAST FAKE HAPPY WORLD

them began to close behind him, enchanted and entrapping him with her. He pushed off, but she held tight, hexing eyes staring into his own eyes behind the helmet. He pushed back again, hitting the surrounding cloth of restraint.

"Look at me, barbarian!" Hexcera struggled. "Lay with me!"

Kalanog gave a final, violent push off and pushed through the enchanted seams of her cloak, coming backward and onto his feet again.

Hexcera lay at the bed before him, though not the same. The black fur of the cloak covered her, not just as a mere blanket, but as a demonic skin. The pathetic witch was now drenched in her own evil, a furred creature, gaping at him with lost, empty eyes.

"Don't go," she begged. "Don't leave me like this, barbarian..."

"What are you becoming, you foul woman?" Kalanog demanded at her strange appearance. "Answer me now, before I slay you like the others!"

She reached for him, a devil's claw, and he stepped away.

"Please," she continued in her struggle to reconnect, "please, stay here with me longer. You have to save me..."

Kalanog looked down at her with pity. "Save you? That's what you want, witch? I would gladly liberate you, but that is not your heart's desire."

"What are you talking about?" she demanded, her same voice emanating from the form of the furred beast. "Of course I want it, I'm trapped in this castle!"

Kalanog surveyed the room, alert and ready for danger.

"You say that your magic shields this castle from invaders," he explained to her, "yet I arrived uninvited and unwelcomed. Your magic is the creation of your shrouding night!"

"Never!"

"It consumes you!" Kalanog roared back to silence her. "Look into the mirror, look what you've become. If I lay with you, it will consume me as well."

Hexcera said nothing, the resentment welling in the beast's eyes.

LAST FAKE HAPPY WORLD

"I will not throw myself to your demons while you sit up here and allow them to exist. I will not, even with all of my might, be able to destroy what you continue to create. Your night never ends because you are too selfish to allow it."

"What will you do then?" she asked with weakening rage. "What will you tell those pathetic villagers who paid you to come here?"

"There were no villagers," Kalanog revealed. "Every villager in reach of your endless suffering has left, you pushed everyone who was ever close to you away with this. I came here on my own accord, I came here carrying a futile wish to help you."

Hexcera was confused, now on her monstrous knees at the floor. The barbarian Kalanog removed his skull helmet and looked to her. His face was that of her forgotten love, from a world away and a left-behind lifetime ago.

"I once loved you," he told her, "but your wickedness pushed me away as well. I traveled here to save you. I nearly died every step of the way, but I lied and told you that my path was easy. I did all of this, only to learn that you won't allow yourself to be saved."

"How can you say that??" Hexcera cried to him. "I've been alone here for so long! I'm trapped in here!"

As they spoke, shadowy figures began lurking in the corners, moving shapes and low sounds.

"I had to see it with my own eyes, but now I see it is the truth. It has completely consumed you. For every one of your demons that is defeated, you cannot resist but to create another. You craft, relish and revel in your misery, expecting others to save you from yourself. So, then, for your sake, I will see this quest through."

Hexcera cried in her furred monster form, her head buried in her arms and a cursed mess of who she used to be.

"It seems impossible, but there is a solution here," the barbarian offered. "What will save you is also the only pleasure that you are now capable of giving me."

LAST FAKE HAPPY WORLD

Hexcera lifted her demonic head from her arms, seeing her long ago lover approaching as her executioner, bringing down his heavy battle axe into her fragile neck.

Kalanog walked the long pathway alone through the woods, no plaguing demons to attack him, no conjured monsters standing in his way. At last, the undying night had ended. A new day was on the horizon, lighting the barbarian's body covered in scars, old and new.

And not far behind him, Hexcera's castle was now collapsing in ruin. Both sides were finally at peace, and he would never look back again.

LAST FAKE HAPPY WORLD

Yessica Doll

Sitting in the car, Lauren Ichbon hesitated in the passenger seat. Certainly, she was attractive, she knew she was. Medium length wild-green hair, deep wild-green eyes. Long legs for an average-height girl, fishnet stockings, a torn black fabric skirt and black strapped boots. Her pushup bra teamed with a red and black corset to overflow her illusion cup size. She had given him all the signs of interest, stopping just shy of grabbing him by his face and plugging her lips into his.

What was it then? She was always confident, but this made her weak. No interest. No signs of desire. What was his name even? Maybe he had told her already, she couldn't remember if he did, and it would sound too weird to ask him now...

Lauren glanced over as he just played with the radio, picking songs from his CDs, dark rock and roll from some country overseas. They sat with no words as the streetlights shined through the dirty windshield, parked outside of the friend's apartment she was staying at.

"I had fun tonight," she offered, the boy in black offering a half smile back. "They were so great."

Nothing. It was killing her. A shared interest, a concert she had traveled across the state to see, a concert that this boy had gone to as well. She had secretly hoped to meet someone at the show, and as soon as her eyes met him, she was trapped. A loner ignoring the pretty girls. He ignored the boys too, so he couldn't be gay. Or could he? Maybe he had a girlfriend already, or a wife?

Lauren breathed, this wasn't like her to get so flustered over a guy. Back home, the boys fell all over her and she could be with anyone she liked. But this, was it the challenge, the surprise of rejection? No not yet, she hadn't been *officially* rejected by him.

Lost in thought and the foreign music, she quickly realized the unnamed boy was now facing her, for who knew how long.

LAST FAKE HAPPY WORLD

"This is her apartment, then?" his baritone voice asked her, a suggestion for her to get out of the car more than a question.

"Yep!" she responded too quickly, smiling too easily. "I didn't expect to be home so early tonight..."

Lauren left her words hanging, letting the sentence linger for him to maybe make a suggestion. Nothing. At the concert, small talk had filled the spaces between songs. He seemed to show interest when she showed interest, at least a physical attraction. Was he shy now, alone with her here? He had jumped at the opportunity to drive her home when she asked, but the entire car ride had been just music and directions.

"My friend's a night owl," Lauren continued her one-sided flirtation. "She probably won't be home for hours."

The bait was out there, but he wasn't biting. This was almost an insult now, maybe he genuinely was just a nice guy who drove her home from the concert? Their eyes crossed paths for a moment, in a brief second of silence on the CD, and everything felt awkward for Lauren then. She went in for the sitting-hug or a passionate kiss, getting the 'just friends' hug in return.

She held it for as long as she could, her corset against his leather jacket at an uncomfortable angle. Once he drove away, she knew that she wouldn't see him again.

"Thanks for the ride," she purred embarrassingly into his ear, the smell of his body stirring her insides.

"Not a problem," he rumbled back into her ear, his voice melting her heart with its ferocity.

Lauren at last let go, pulling away just a bit though still leaning in. Close enough for a kiss, close enough to be scared to breathe. Nothing, failure. She sank in her defeat, pulling back into the passenger side and taking a last look at him. Black leather coat, fishnet shirt and chains, black spiked hair, tattoos down his neck and the piercings... She didn't meet boys like this often, and it was difficult to say goodbye.

But it was time to go now, into her friend's empty apartment all alone. Time to let the night end, sleep and head back home on the train tomorrow.

"Ok," she conceded, "goodnight, stranger..."

"Goodnight," he replied and added not a single word more.

Lauren opened the car door and slowly stepped out, out into the lonely night and stood wallowing in her own emptiness. Screw it, if she would never see him again, then one last shot.

"You know," she began as she leaned down into the view of the car interior, "you could make a girl do anything you want."

She couldn't believe her own audacity, but this was all or nothing. She was used to always having her way, and she was acting in uncharted territory now. Before he showed any sort of reaction, she quickly upped the stakes and rephrased her surprise proclamation.

"What I mean is, you could make *me* do anything you want."

"...Is that right?" he asked, a different flavor in his voice this time around. Maybe something in him had cracked, somehow Lauren finding a secret shortcut through his bulletproof defense.

"Yeah," she replied.

"Yeah?" he returned her reply, both at the standstill of 'what now then.'

Lauren took the initiative before this sudden opportunity passed, coming back into the car and slamming the passenger door a little too aggressively. She met him in a forced kiss that was mostly her, but no matter. This was a victory for her faltering ego and she reveled in it. He was so strange to her still, even now. His hands didn't wander like a usual boy, she opened her eyes in the kiss and saw that his remained open, staring back with curious excitement.

"Anything?" he asked as the kiss took a break, lips but a small breath apart.

"Yeah, anything you want," she bragged and tempted, trusting his unknown limits versus her imagination. "How bad could you possibly be?"

"Ok, then," he said in a business-like tone and pulled away from

LAST FAKE HAPPY WORLD

the closeness, putting his hand into an inside pocket of his coat.

As he reached, she watched the muscle of his body beneath the fishnet. Pectorals and abs. The attraction for her was surreal and she couldn't wait to kiss him again, to bring him upstairs and be locked away from the world together.

A smile spread across his handsome face, his strong jaw and cheeks. She had found a way to get control now, it had only been a matter of time.

"What's that?" Lauren asked, the boy pulling a black flask from his coat.

"It's time to celebrate," he grinned as he twisted off its metallic top, a coiled dragon like a snake.

Lauren grinned along with him, looking curiously at her new friend. "What is it?"

"Well, you said that you would do anything for me, right? So then start with this. Goat blood."

Lauren laughed hard at his humor.

"Sure, it is," she played along. "Because you totally just keep a flask of animal blood in your coat."

"I do."

"You are so goth," she taunted him, taking the flask from his hands with absolute doubt.

It smelled of iron and another strange thing she couldn't place. Probably a cheap alcohol he had snuck into the concert. With a roll of her eyes, she brought it to her lips and tilted her head back. It poured like warm lava into her mouth, its foul and acidic taste. The mouthful she swallowed hard, looking across at the pleasantly pleased boy.

"Too strong?" he joyfully mocked her reaction, reaching back for the container.

"No, no," she lied, licking the air from the horrid taste. "I'm a big girl, I can handle it."

He expressed approval as Lauren tilted her head back again, eager to impress him. She let the alcoholic blood pour through her mouth, skipping the taste this time and letting it flow directly into her throat. Every drop, she would show him. Now that she had a chance, she was going to live it up. No rules, party hard tonight and leave for home tomorrow. This meeting was turning out to be everything she had been hoping it would be.

"Impressive," he complimented her, taking the empty flask back and marveling at her action. "You weren't lying, were you? It looks like tonight is going to be interesting after all."

Lauren sunk into the passenger seat with a victorious look. She was feeling half seductive and half... disoriented.

Her eyes felt odd, unfocused and slipping. Was he driving again? But she had wanted to bring him upstairs...

"Everything's alright," he calmed her, reaching across and aiding with her seatbelt.

Lauren went to talk, but her words didn't form the things she wanted to say. She felt relaxed and confused, wanting to fall asleep but knowing something was wrong. The music was on still but louder now, his window was down, and the wind was soothing. She leaned toward him and rested her head on his shoulder, his physical smell so intoxicating still.

And her thoughts drifted away.

There was a breeze that blew by, blowing her green hair around like leaves in a tree. Every muscle in her body felt weak as she opened her swollen eyes, seeing in a drunk and unfocused sight the city skyline, so beautiful at night. The strange boy was sitting beside her, out of the car, their legs hanging over the edge of something.

"Where are we?" Lauren coughed and asked in a sleepy voice. "What happened to me..."

"You fell asleep, little mouse," he quietly told her. "Nothing to worry about. Isn't this a view?"

In her groggy waking, she attempted to look around. There was his car, that black thorn in the night, parked behind them with the headlights on. Where was this?

"A parking garage, the top floor of the hospital parking garage," he told her, almost as if he could read her thoughts. "We're just killing time. I always wondered - If you jump off and die, do they take you inside the hospital, or straight to the mortuary? I used to drop action figures off my dresser when I was a kid, I pretended they were falling to their deaths."

He continued talking and Lauren lost her connection with reality. His words blurred and began to soothe her into a dangerous slumber cycle. She tried to recognize her inability to control herself, but the focus was going. Something was wrong now, she looked lifelessly down at the hospital grounds and entrance maybe five long stories below. This was so dangerous to sit here like this, she prayed she didn't fall and tried to hold her dark friend, fading out again, lost in a poisoned sleep.

Lauren vaguely felt the rumble of the car later, the vibration of the engine as she fell in and out of awareness. The fear of falling from that parking garage replayed in her stream of laced-dream thoughts, a nightmare until she shook and came awake. The car, it had stopped and was parked now. The headlights were shining down an alley, her unusual friend out in front and conversing with a stranger.

She sat motionless, fighting to see, her eyes zooming in and out. Lauren felt sick with the eye strain, something deeper than a migraine headache pounding her skull into a sweat. There was movement ahead, a glance by both figures back at the vehicle, or more specifically back at her. Her eyelids hovered and dipped, uncontrollably about to shut. The dark boy made his way back to the idle car while the stranger opened a doorway in the alley.

Asleep in thoughts, with nothing making sense. Every time Lauren's mind became alert, her body shut down and fell back into

LAST FAKE HAPPY WORLD

an uneasy, restless sleep. There was no vibration of the car this time, no music and no breeze. The sounds of talking, or was that in a dream? Back asleep, no control at all.

"Why don't you have a seat?" the comforting voice of the dark boy suggested.

Lauren felt her body being helped into a soft, sitting position, then the sights unveiled as she became aware. Stuffed animals?

"How did we... get here?" she managed in a voice that was close to a whisper.

"We walked, silly. You don't remember that?"

In these brief moments of an abbreviated awareness, it became apparent to Lauren that she was not constantly falling asleep, she was losing control of memory and blacking in and out. She could remember walking from the car into the building now, but at the same time she couldn't *really* remember... It was the effects of the goat blood, or whatever drug it really was. The correlation of mind and body still wasn't working, but she tried in these moments to pull herself out of the controlling state.

"Why am I in here?" she struggled to ask, looking all around in a desperate disarray.

It was an elevated box or container, filled and surrounding her with cheap and brightly colored stuffed animals.

"Why not?" the boy asked her back as he closed a window-like glass panel. "It's just for a little bit, it'll be fun. You're a real prize after all, aren't you?"

Now Lauren was closed in, her body so tired that she could barely lift a finger. Two other strange people walked up alongside the dark boy, standing there watching her through the glass. The boy then took something from his pocket, a coin, and leaned down to insert it below.

Lights came on in the glass box, music too, and up above a mechanical claw swung to life, moving from right to left.

A claw machine?

LAST FAKE HAPPY WORLD

The small claw stopped and dropped down, landing on her body and pinching at her fishnet stockings. They were already torn in places, but the claw grabbed and pulled upward, tearing them again.

"Aww, man!" one of the unknown boys complained. "You almost had her! Let me try!"

Lauren lay there helpless, dazed as the boys took turns. The claw machine claw grabbed and tore at her clothing repeatedly, rising to drop small fragments into the prize chute, then dropping to scratch at her exhausted body again.

Lauren couldn't comprehend or even fight this perverted game, falling into her ongoing blackout as her clothing was picked apart.

"And she said to me, 'you can make me do anything you want,' can you believe it??"

The boy's familiar voice was the same yet stronger, followed by a small chorus of laughs. She opened her eyes and then took in a glimpse of the room, filled with dozens of lights and unfocused shapes.

"Oh, look!" a new voice filled with glee marveled. "Your doll awakens!"

One of the shapes came up to her closely, all of the way until eyes met eyes and said to her "Can you speak? Tell me your name, doll?"

"I'm Lauren..." she answered, the claw machine now vague in her fuzzy memory. "What happened... to me..."

"Very funny, Yessica," the voice responded, the person's head pulling back a bit and into a temporary focus, the furry mask of a rabbit head staring at her now. "You have such an unrealistic body, Yessica! Look at you! That's not what a real girl even looks like!"

Lauren looked away from the strange, cartoon rabbit mask and down to her body. Her neck hardly turned, moving in a slow, hard plastic movement. Her entire body felt odd and pressed in plastic, almost encased in a medical cast.

"Allow me to show you, Yessica," the dark boy who had brought her here told her, walking into sight.

He brought a body-length mirror toward her, then holding it up so she could see herself, his own lecherous face peering over the top at her reaction.

What in the world was this now? It truly was a cast, a hard-plastic, see-through body cast that entrapped her now naked body. Makeup was painted on its face, with holes for her eyes, mouth and nostrils.

"What... is it??" Lauren cried as she stood there helplessly on display. "What did you... do to me??"

"What's the matter?" he asked from behind the mirror. "Look at you, you're almost exactly the doll I was looking for! The body type isn't an exact fit, and your tits turned out to be a bit smaller without those bra tricks you were using, but you look great! Like a perfect, mass-market doll!"

Lauren cried more, standing there in dread. "I can't move..."

"Aww, sure you can," the boy reassured her and set the mirror aside. "Your doll-casing is articulated in eleven places. Even your knees, some doll lines don't get articulated knees. With practice, you might eventually be able to walk around on your own, kind of. Yessica – Whoa, Yessica, we're losing you again... Hello?"

Between terrors and confused fear, Lauren passed out into her dreaded blackout slumber again. She felt her plastic-encased body tip and almost fall, coming to a slow stop as if someone had set her down on the floor.

When she came to again, Lauren was propped up with her back against a wall, her returning eyesight revealing the obscene room in full detail. There were so many people there, all naked and in strange masks just like the rabbit. They went about conversation and mingling as if she were an afterthought, hardly a look sent her way. The oddness of it all was sinking in. Sight after sight was nonsensical now and had been ever since she drank that blood.

A small amount of strength was returning, and with a little effort, she summoned the energy to tip forward from the wall.

And she took her first steps.

Like a stiff, animated doll, she slowly scissor-walked around the scene of deviant characters and worse acts. Naked people with hidden faces. Dogs, rats and other masks. Lauren walked with a clumsy stride into walls and tables, rebounding and recovering. There were conversations she overheard about unconventional things, quantum tunneling and quantum resurrection, unpopular topics like the Black Mass and Unit 731, but most of all and oddly enough, conversations about toys.

"Feeling all better, Yessica?"

The familiar voice of the dark boy came from a black goat mask and naked body, the telltale tattoos running down his neck.

"Why do you keep... calling me that..." Lauren asked her confusing abductor.

He walked behind her and put his arms around her hard-plastic body.

"Because that's your name. 'Yessica, the doll that won't say no!' More or less, you gave yourself to me, remember? It's almost like I put the words in your mouth."

She stood in silence, unable to see him there behind her and against her, instead just helplessly staring forward.

"Ever since I was a kid, I've always loved toys," he went on, playing with and manipulating her stiff arms. "In fact, this building that we're in used to be my favorite toy store. But that was before it went bankrupt and eventually out of business. No need for sad stories now, you're right here for me to play with. And you can still live your life just like a real girl. You can kind of walk, you can kind of talk. Your doll casing even has all of the necessary holes for all of your necessary holes, Yessica."

This reality was too much to take, the horrible dark boy running

LAST FAKE HAPPY WORLD

his hands across the transparent plastic over her body. Lauren was feeling weaker still, leaning back and almost falling, then passing in and out again.

The familiar feeling of uncontrolled motion came across her, but not in his car again. She was being carried this time, as if truly a giant toy, her body sweating in the humidity of the casing.

Now she was set down, alert again and the stiff plastic suit put in a sitting position. There was a chair she was set on and makeshift cardboard walls to the left and right, the shadow of a miniature cardboard roof overhead.

"When I was young," the boy said from a seat beside her, "I only had toys that boys had. Action figures, monsters, robots, the usual boy stuff. But I remember getting my first 'girl's doll,' I kind of stole it from my sister's room."

"Just let me go…"

"Please, be quiet…The popular 'Yessica doll,' my sister had so many, she never even knew I took it. I included it in all of my role playing, she was kidnapped and rescued, dropped off from castle walls and sometimes almost eaten alive. I won't even tell you what I did with her beneath my blankets."

A bear-masked person then walked up toward the sitting pair, standing before their cardboard walls.

"This is a kissing booth, Yessica," the dark boy told her. "I would always make my doll be friendly with every monster toy I had. It made me so happy, I know you're going to love it too."

"No -" Lauren tried to cry but was silenced, the shaggy mask of the bear pressing his mouth against hers through the mouth hole of her encased head.

She fought back with her teeth to no avail, biting in small defense but she was still so powerless inside. The bear mask continued to press against her, a foul taste of it and soon the only energy she had left was used for the ongoing struggle to breathe.

LAST FAKE HAPPY WORLD

"Ooh, very nice," the boy observed. "But don't take up too much time now, bear! There are plenty of more monsters waiting in line behind you!"

As the bear man stepped away and aside at last, Lauren saw that it was true. As much as her eyes could see, there was in fact a waiting line of the masked people behind him.

One by one they approached as she lost all will. She fought back with tiny bites here and there, but eventually struggled to even manipulate her mouth. Kiss after kiss and worse, violation after violation, in and out of this torturously aware state.

In the abuse she faded out, the world in this abandoned toy store falling away at once. Between dreams and reality, she drifted briefly, almost clinging to the sleep and afraid to open her eyes ever again.

Lauren woke, set crookedly on the floor like a doll that had fallen from a shelf, her mouth sore and her body sweating profusely. Slowly she looked around, it was still reality. The more details her mind could process now, the increasingly vile their nakedness became. Old flesh of men, the stretched flesh of women. The memories of the kissing booth were already fading in her mind, her chapped lips cracked in broken dryness.

"Why... I don't understand why I'm here..."

"You really don't?" the goat-masked boy stood over her and asked, an imitation in his wording. "I'm only playing with you. We're all just playing with you. You gave yourself to me, Yessica, like a brand-new toy. You're a damaged, carbon copy Yessica doll for me to collect. And I'll play with you until I get bored, or until you break, or until I find one in better condition."

Lauren couldn't handle it. The abduction, the sexuality with these strangers, the confinement of this plastic exoskeleton.

"I'm not a doll," she tried to scream, instead the words coming out softly from her tired lungs. "I'm not a doll..."

Tears ran down her face and stuck between the plastic and her

LAST FAKE HAPPY WORLD

cheek. She tried her arms and then her hands again. Nothing.

The boy bent down and leaned in to see her, removing the goat mask from his head.

"Are you done being my toy, Yessica?" he asked with a bizarre look in his eyes. "Are you done bending to my will?"

"Yes..." she sobbed, unable to control herself. "Yes... Please, yes..."

Sounds of the gathering's revelry filled her ears as she clenched her tearful eyes and then tried not to open them again. The blackout was falling upon her one last time, leaving the broken Lauren no choice but to openly embrace it.

She felt the rumble of his car engine once more.

"I never told you what my name was," his voice penetrated the darkness. "I may not be your creator, but I am the hand that brought you to life. I was your master, the imagination that made your plastic body matter. I don't think you'll ever realize this, but when you gave yourself to me, you threw yourself away. You were already a broken toy when I got you. I did my part. I entertained myself, and then I left my garbage by the street."

Lauren Ichbon looked around in the emptiness, her senses were coming back, all the dark events going away. Rotten smells, textures and a blocked vision. It was trash and she could feel she was still encased in plastic, cramped in a small space and her doll body covered in waste. Old banana peels, empty cans, wrappers and moldy bread.

She managed to push with her plastic arms, the walls of her tiny confinement stretching, but stretching what? It was a bag wall, a garbage bag surrounding her. Her stiff hands pressed through, finally puncturing a small escape to the freedom she had sought.

Her doll eyes peeked out, peering through the torn hole like a keyhole back to her real world.

LAST FAKE HAPPY WORLD

It was nighttime in the cool air of the outside, and she found her body abandoned on the expressway. The garbage bag had been dropped and disposed of cruelly in the middle lane, vehicles of drunken people racing home from their wild weekend night.

Helpless and without a scream, the blinding light of a semitruck plowed through the bag, blasting pieces of garbage - as well as plastic pieces of a broken Yessica doll - into the air and night.

Follow Me Down

There was an expected knock at the front door, and though he didn't know who it was specifically, he knew the type of person it would be in a situation like this.

"Hi, Alex," an attractive woman in a professional suit-dress greeted. "I'm Mrs. Breit, I'm with the -"

"I know who you're with," he informed her. "Feel free to come in, I know why you're here."

She headed into the front room of the quiet house, adjusting her black framed glasses and pushing her golden locks of hair back behind her shoulders.

"So," she said with an attempt to open communication, "I see that you're already well under way here!"

Alex gave her a sincere smile, heading back through his house to continue with the business at hand. Boxes were stacked neatly, placed against the walls and packed with his belongings. The lady followed, taking written notes on a clipboard of everything she could see.

"What's all that for?" Alex questioned her without hostility, going to an already-open refrigerator door.

"For the studies," she answered, her hand still taking notes. "I'm not just here to help you, I'm here to learn so we can help others like you in the future."

Alex continued with his task, removing all items from the refrigerator and freezer, putting them into a large garbage bag at the floor.

"You weren't hungry, were you?" he asked the woman, feeling oddly guilty throwing out so much food in front of someone.

She continued jotting down whatever note she was writing, then looking up and unaware of the question.

"I asked if you were hungry," Alex repeated. "I feel bad throwing it out if you want something."

LAST FAKE HAPPY WORLD

"Oh, no, I'm good, thank you!"

"Let me guess," he said as he returned to the freezer, throwing out unused pizza and other things he had purchased. "On a diet?"

"Of course, how did you guess?" she answered in an automatic way. "I have to look my best, you know."

"It seems like everyone's always on a diet. Say," he paused as he closed off the garbage bag, "what's your name, anyway?"

"I already told you. Mrs. Breit."

"No, no... What's your first name? Who are you, Mrs. Breit?"

There was a time lapse where she looked at him curiously, as if no one in this type of situation had ever asked her what her name was.

"...It's Samantha," she answered with a slight strain on her face, confused why he would care.

"Ok, Samantha. Listen to me, you really don't need to diet. You look perfectly fine the way that you are, even though I'm sure everyone already tells you things like that."

And some did, but it felt strange for her to hear it from him. Wasn't he supposed to be crying? Or depressed? Why was this one acting so complimentary and positive?

She collected her thoughts and followed the man through his home, returning to her notes. Every framed photo from the wall was removed, every item in each room neatly packed away. There were hardly any more signs of his presence in this house that he would very shortly be leaving behind.

"Um, so, did you call the electric company?" she asked, trying to return to her professional demeanor.

"Yep."

"Ok, the phone company? What about the cable?"

"Yes, and yes. Everything's in order, everything is canceled and being turned off."

"The post office?"

"Yes again," Alex grinned as if she should know. "I instructed them to stop delivering."

LAST FAKE HAPPY WORLD

"Well, you've definitely covered all of your bases," Samantha sighed with relief. "You're making my job way too easy."

"Then relax," he suggested. "There's nothing that important going on, you can just talk to me."

Despite his strange suggestion, Samantha Breit tried to remain semi-professional. She tailed him through the emptying of the house, the throwing away and the remaining packing-up of things. All the meanwhile, he tried to joke and break through her seriousness to only small success.

"And now the part I've been dreading the most," he announced with a slight mumble, heading to the back door.

Samantha watched as Alex called to his pets, two dogs and a cat, kneeling down to talk to them. He kissed them on their heads and hugged them, saying his goodbyes and telling them that he loved them. The door opened and they ran away, out to live their lives in the world without him.

"You ok?" Samantha asked a few seconds after he closed the door again. "I know some goodbyes are difficult."

"We had a great time together. I really love those guys."

By now, nearly all the things that needed to be done were done. Everything was canceled, everything was off. Everything was packed and now the pets had been released.

"So," Samantha stood up straight and prepared for the finale, "do you have any last words?"

"No, not yet," he answered, not surprised by the question but surprising her with his answer.

"Oh! Well, we, um, we can wait a little if you want, but... Sometimes prolonging it only makes it more difficult. If it's because of the pills, we can choose another method. You didn't specify on the paperwork how you wanted to go."

"No, it's not about waiting, and it's not about the pills, either. I'm actually not using any of the methods you provide."

"But it's stated on the forms that you're done. You... You have to do it."

LAST FAKE HAPPY WORLD

Nervousness vibrated through her voice. She had been trained to deal with things very similar to this, but for some reason she was at a loss for this specific reaction.

"So, then..."

"So, then what?" he asked back, seeing the confusion in her face.

"So then if you're not going to kill yourself, are you... In love again? Or are you ready to look for love again?? If so that's great, but..."

Alex gave a small shake of his head and walked to the front door, ready to walk away from it all. Samantha Breit was flustered, standing there with her heart pounding as he seemed to be disobeying procedure.

"Well, which one??" she begged. "Please, which one is it?"

Alex opened the door and turned back, looking at her with absolute indifference in his eyes. "Neither," he proclaimed, then walking through the door.

The world outside of his house was an extraordinary world in some ways. People lived and loved, worked and died, their lives ruled by timepieces and affection. They sold their lifetime by working hourly to the highest bidder, then spent the remaining pocket change of time on love. It was Valentine's Day every day here and the entire town was love struck, decorated in pinks and heart shapes on every corner. Stores sold flowers and cards, chocolates and stuffed animals.

It was inescapable and absorbing, Alex never being able to figure out if these people worshipped clocks or hearts. Now no longer caring, he walked the streets one last time in his favorite jeans, his favorite shirt and his favorite hat. All around him were the fragrances of perfumes and colognes. Pop songs played from passing cars and their radios, every song about love and indirect mating rituals. Lingerie shops popped up on streets, mixed in like

LAST FAKE HAPPY WORLD

you wouldn't see, and in dark corners, adult shops for romance of all designs.

"Alex!" the lady's voice called to him from behind. "Please wait! Where are you going??"

He didn't answer, but his walking pace allowed for her brisk jog to catch up. She came to his side, matching stride as he marched onward down the street.

"Alex! Please! Talk to me, what are you doing?"

"Why does it matter?" he asked. "Your work is finished, you can go home now. Do I really have to kill myself for your job to be justified?"

"Well, actually," she wondered out loud, "I kind of think you do. I mean, every time I get sent out, that's what happens... That's why I'm there."

"Samantha," he said with a deep breath, "just walk with me, alright?"

She hesitated and then nodded, walking side by side with him as an odd matching pair.

"Look around us," he asked of her. "What are we doing with our lives?"

She clung to her clipboard and didn't have an answer, not quite understanding what he was asking.

"This town," he continued, "these people... Everyone's either in love or they're heartbroken. Some of the people married here don't even like each other. Everyone's on a date or looking for a date. Every song is about love, good or bad, some way or the other."

"Love is everything to us," Samantha said in a serious voice. "Love is what we live for in this town, without it we have nothing."

They walked down the road, Alex looking one last time with unfiltered eyes.

"Love is pretty good," he agreed with his companion. "It's not everything, though. I assume you're married, *Mrs*. Breit?"

LAST FAKE HAPPY WORLD

"Yes, of course! I love my husband more than anything."

"Then that's wonderful, I'm extremely happy for you. But what about someone like me? If I'm not in love, what am I supposed to do with my life?"

"You know what you're supposed to do... Are you really asking me, like you actually want me to tell you?"

"Sure, why not?"

"Well, you meet someone. You date. Maybe you get engaged, maybe get married. Maybe there are kids later..."

"Yeah, I get that, but what if it doesn't quite work out the way that it's supposed to?"

"Then you try again, Alex."

"Ok, I tried a few times and it was fun. But our existence in this town somehow became only about love and how to pursue it. I don't care anymore about these things."

"Right," Samantha agreed, "and then you're heartbroken. You pursue a new love when the time comes, when you're ready to move on."

"And then a new love, and then another new love and so on and so on, until death you depart."

"Sir," Samantha took a long, deep breath and returned to her professional dialog, "you live and love, or you die trying. When your status changes, you start over. Every year, you renew your love license. If you're late, there's a grace period. If you're loveless, our government offers classes to retrain you. However, people such as yourself, who continue to miss their renewal date, must file 'love hardship' paperwork."

"I did all of that."

"Precisely. Which is why I was sent to aid in your suicide. It's perfectly natural to kill yourself over a love hardship, it's nothing to be ashamed of."

"I'm not going to do things the way that I'm expected to."

"So…. What then? You're going to look for love again? If you are, I can put in a request to cancel the paperwork and -"

LAST FAKE HAPPY WORLD

"Sam, stop talking. You sound like a robot."

That name, it felt strange hearing a stranger say it. That was the name her husband called her, the nickname her parents used when she was growing up. And now here this stranger said it, as if he were someone close to her.

"Everything you're saying is what they tell you to say," Alex criticized. "Love isn't supposed to be work, and work isn't supposed to be life. If it's natural, that's great. But why am I supposed to spend my life looking for something I might not even want? What if I find it, and then it leaves me when I'm old? What was the point of everything then?"

They walked on together, and though it was sacrilege to her ears, she tried to listen to the things he said. They saw the Valentine's Day town and its people as they traveled towards the center. Hearts everywhere and the same familiar faces, a few faces of the women he had dated, and even a few of the ones Samantha had dated once upon a time as well.

"Good to see you again," Alex called out to one as they passed. "Good luck with everything!"

Her reaction was stupefied, as if he shouldn't be talking to her, or since he was, maybe that he was interested in her one more time again.

A few people began to follow the odd pair out of curiosity. Samantha's suit-dress was a uniform that signaled a suicide worker, but why was she walking so nonchalantly with him outdoors?

"I hope you buy a lot of clothes that you love!" he waved at an ex-girlfriend, then turning to whisper to Samantha. "She left me for some guy with a lot of money. He had a horrible personality, but she really loved that money."

"You must hate her," she whispered back.

"Not really. At first, I was really defeated, you know? What a blow to my self-esteem. But it's what she wanted, so why not? I'm sure she's much happier now."

LAST FAKE HAPPY WORLD

By now, the curious followers were building up in a small number. Suicides were an everyday thing in the love-based town, but seldom was a suicide case seen out wandering with their government worker. Some followed in wonder, others out of a morbid fascination, and still others out of flock mentality.

Through the town and down the road, surrounded by bright colors and cartoon heart balloons. There were weddings in the park by the fountain, blind dates meeting up for an afternoon lunch, even a proposal by two quite attractive people. As the center of the town drew near, Samantha began to suspect Alex's ultimate destination.

"Are you heading where I think you are?"

"What if I am?"

"Well, I mean if you are, that's fine, but why would you?"

There was only a blank look and a shaking of the head from Alex, walking on and shortly coming upon the end of his road. There were faded 'do-not-enter' signs and 'authorized personal only' warnings. The people that followed slowed down, still watching but lingering as closely as they were legally allowed to. Alex continued, a fleeting look over his shoulder as he knew they wouldn't follow.

"Hey! You can't go in there! Alex!"

He disregarded Samantha's shouts of authority and continued the short distance.

It was a giant hole in the ground, a 'bottomless pit' in the center of the city. Every generation had used this as their place to throw away the past. Old, unsalvageable cars were pushed in by authorized workers. Funerals took place with the dead bodies afterwards dropped into the depths. Garbage, old technology, clothes, furniture and everything that was once used or important was thrown into the pit, left to yesterday and never to be seen again.

LAST FAKE HAPPY WORLD

"Alex, you can't stand so close to it!" Samantha yelled as she crossed the restricted lines. "Even I'm not supposed to be in here! Stop goofing around!"

She approached him as he stood at the edge. It was as wide as a small lake, birds diving and rising in and out, the infinite blackness of their discarded past before them. Alex looked down and saw nothing, then turning back and seeing the followers standing there. There were strangers and people he may have someday met. The former girlfriends with their new love failures and successes. And they all watched the alien scene of a man simply walking away.

"*Alex*!" Samantha tried again, pulling at his arm while eyeing the black hole.

"Everyone listen to me!" Alex shouted out, loud enough so that the small crowd could hear him. "I know this isn't going to make sense to most of you, but at least try to listen. I'm not in love, but I'm not heartbroken either. I know that some of you are very happy, and that's great. Maybe some of you are in bad relationships, who knows, maybe it'll work itself out. But I found a way to live outside of that. I'm not depressed, but I'm not interested in a new love either."

A few heads turned, confusion already spreading across their faces.

"Each of us used to be happy before we started worrying about love or time," he continued. "Everything we've thrown away, everything that we used to be is down here, in this bottomless pit. I want to be surrounded by the things I used to value, I want to leave this unending distraction of everyday-love behind. I've reached a point in my existence where I'd rather rediscover yesterday than look forward to tomorrow."

No one understood the words he said, and Samantha stopped tugging at his arm.

"You can come too, if you want," he offered, "but I'm ok with going alone. One day, all of you will head into a version of this

LAST FAKE HAPPY WORLD

darkness too. You'll lose those loved ones no matter how much money you save, no matter what you say or do. It'll be through their choice or yours, and if not that, one of you will lose the other in death. Eventually, we all leave, one way or the other. So, I'm leaving now, to meet my fate without love or misery. You can follow me down if you want to."

It was a flash in time, Samantha reaching for him as he stepped off, but it was futile. Alex left the game of love and fell happily into the pit of discarded days gone by. It was terrifying at first, to be falling alone deeper. Everything was black as the safety of the controlled world above lost its reach of light. Falling fast and it felt great, the rush of air leaving him exhilarated after the first stage of fear went away.

His eyes began to see. There were old things and even older things together. He fell through built up clogging levels of garbage bags and bodies, water and rain cascading through like unnatural and makeshift waterfalls. Land on a layer, look around and fall through a layer, pieces of yesterday breaking loose and then descending with him. Alex saw thrown away toys that brought back great memories, board game boxes and book covers from his youth that he had somehow forgotten about.
And there were people too. It was bittersweet, but he saw the faces of people long since passed, stuck in the pit's dirt wall as he fell past them quickly. Family members, people of before, forgotten to yesterday but now remembered again. It was only in small glimpses, but for a moment they were with him once more. Yesterday was racing back to him as he traveled down to somewhere new.

The end would come eventually, nothing lasts forever and even a bottomless pit eventually meets its end. But Alex made sure to cherish every moment as he plummeted through to the unknown

LAST FAKE HAPPY WORLD

world. With the joy of his nostalgic rediscoveries, even the smallest fear of being alone fell away as he plunged into the obscure abyss, brilliantly racing toward the inevitable expiration that we all one day would face.

The world forgot about Alex, and Alex forgot about the world.

LAST FAKE HAPPY WORLD

Dangerous Distractions

Another day of bored luxury drifted by, blurring sunny yesterday into a sunny today, next into an inescapable sunny tomorrow. The Lady Marlissa was surrounded by her invited friends and their stranger friends, all dying to stay and thrilled to death to spend their afternoons-into-nights at her manor.

"I said to him," Lady Marlissa continued her story, "if you should ever desire to be my lover again, you will have to wait one thousand afternoons and one thousand nights."

"And what did he reply?"

Marlissa smiled. "The fool looked me dead in the eye, feigned intelligence and whispered then to me - 'I would wait those two thousand days and longer.' Can you believe that? It was only one thousand days, not two!"

A few of the gathered laughed, the others around with their noses buried in hardcover books. Marlissa's smile half wilted intensely at their distractions.

"We made love regardless," she tacked on for shock.

"And where is he now, this simpleton?"

"Who can say?" she coyly replied. "Gone forever, however, wherever. He served his purpose to me."

The day was the same as always. Quiet walks through the garden, rowboats in the pond, lounging about by famous paintings or eating at a table full of desserts. The women wore giant powdered wigs, cleavage-creating corsets and overwhelmingly elaborate dresses, the men in their European suits with peruke wigs and ponytail ribbons.

"The point of existence is... what?" a handsome gentleman wondered out loud.

Lady Marlissa was an elitist among the elite. She made sure that her hair was always taller, her waist smaller and her cleavage more distracting than any woman in her presence. Those that came close were seldom seen again, with no one daring to care why.

"The point of life is simply to eat," Marlissa answered the waiting question, eyeing her silent guests. "The point of life is to indulge one's desires, nothing more."

But even indulgence had its limit in Lady Marlissa's view. The days were changing in society, and she noticed it in her reflective autumn eyes immediately. Gone were the afternoons of laughter and conversation. Every purposely and rewardingly-boring activity she cherished was being ruined by the invention of the 'book.' The technology of 'print.' Everything was tainted by its controlling touch. On every garden stroll, someone had a book held to their face. Pleasant boat rowing would drift ashore by a nose lost in a book. And even at the dining table, more and more guests of hers were reading in place of talking, turning pages left until nothing was right.

Their obsession, with a book in their hand and their neck craned down, repulsed Lady Marlissa to no end. Conversation was still had, in bits, but elation typically came from what one shared with themselves alone. This weakness of the human mind was as inescapable as a moth flying into a candle, and oftentimes Marlissa found herself completely alone while still surrounded by others.

Outside, in the temperate sun of the summertime, Lady Marlissa sat beneath a parasol, looking over the males of the species.

"The point of life is... what?" asked one of the seated men, his eyes looking up from the bound pages of his book.

"You asked that question already," Marlissa replied, staring at him with intentions.

"Did I? I suppose I did, silly me," the man remembered with perplexed and blushing cheeks. "What was the answer then?"

The audacity annoyed Marlissa to no end. She was used to being the center of attention here, not vying for it with words in the hand.

"Indulgence," she repeated with a huff, the man's eyes already

LAST FAKE HAPPY WORLD

down to his novel, or poetry, or whatever he was lost in today.

"Indulgence," he soullessly repeated her repeat, his mind already returning to the pages.

Lady Marlissa stood up from the garden chair abruptly, and with her parasol in hand, she left her group and walked the grounds, taking inventory of her guests and their activities. The air felt good blowing through her oversized wig and silk dress this summer day, but that was all that felt worthwhile. Even boredom was more fulfilling than this nothingness, these simple people she had called her friends at one time or another.

A few passed in the garden, heads down and hardly noticing her.

On to the path around the pond. Rowboats sat still as if ashore, slightly drifting in the breeze. The two onboard were reading a single book, together. Where were the days of not too long ago, with a gentleman on the bench kissing her right hand, a liaison kissing her left hand while concealed in the bushes? Where were the days of lustful wants and unexpected questions? Everyone was so wrapped up, so entangled in their entrapments.

They collectively had one last chance to change her mind.

Marlissa returned to the interior of her manor, now among those who lounged about, reading their tales indoors. She put her parasol away and took a dessert, finding a seat among the distracted. Her eyes took in the entire room, not the familiar decoration but the soon to be unwanted gathering. A few words were said here and there, a few looks and glances, but it was still the mindlessness and mental-distance she abhorred.

This was their final opportunity to entertain her. She cast her sight to a random man, the proximity of his body her sole attraction. While distracted in his reading, sitting alone and across from her, Lady Marlissa pulled her corset top forward and down just enough to slowly expose her breasts. Though not often this random, displays and activities of sexuality were not unheard of here.

LAST FAKE HAPPY WORLD

She watched his eyes dart along the written words of the page, his brain handcuffed like a slave, and this final chance for salvation was coming to an end.

But then a change, and a flash of hope. The young man's face came from a turning page and gasped at the sight of her uncovered upper body. No ink-on-page words could compete with her voluptuous shape, and no spoken words were exchanged as she willed him to join her at the love seat, walking like a fly into its carnivorous plant death.

Here, then. This would redeem them, the pathetic people, if only for one more night.

He sat beside her, nervous and eager, and it filled her mind with the feelings she had lost. Marlissa looked around, no one watched or cared this time, but no matter. She was selfish after all. She tilted her head to the side so that the well-dressed man could kiss below her ear, and just as his tender lips touched her pale skin, a small laugh of breath blew onto her neck.

She waited for his kiss. Another breathing laugh.

"Do I make you nervous?" she asked, anticipating perhaps it was his first time so close to someone like her.

"No," he calmly replied, breathing deeply, "it's just the book I'm reading, there's this hilarious part where -"

He continued as Marlissa stood up. This would be enough then. Though enraged, she walked calmly, breasts still exposed and she couldn't care less. Whatever he had said, she didn't listen, past the reading people she walked, through the halls and toward the kitchen.

"Everyone is staying over, so let's make this a grand feast," Marlissa instructed her male cooks. "The party will continue until tomorrow."

"*Everyone?*" a nerve-wracked servant asked back.

"Yes, everyone this time. It doesn't matter what you prepare, but you know what to include. Am I understood?"

LAST FAKE HAPPY WORLD

As the setting sun spread into the horizon, the guests returned to the manor from the garden and surrounding acre. There was noticeably more socializing this time, but it was too late in Marlissa's eyes. Even the conversations seemed more trivial than usual, or perhaps she was just done with everyone here. By this time in a week or two there would be new people to invite, new romance and new excitements to be bored by. But first she had something long overdue to take care of. Something to indulge in.

"My gathered guests and fellow socialites," she toasted the group at the evening's lavish dinner, "as one of you asked me today, on two occasions, might I add, the point of life is what?"

Though no one answered her rhetorical question, she was impressed to at least have their undivided attention.

"The point of life is simply indulgence," she continued, standing between the two long dining tables. "And tonight, you will each indulge, as will I. Live, eat and love as if there is no tomorrow."

A few small claps as the collection of ungrateful guests dined like unfed hogs. Marlissa watched over them as she took her seat at the head of the master table. What weak-willed fools. Even in gorging themselves, their books were present at the table, some open and others bookmarked, too important to set aside.

"How much should we put out?" one of the cooks whispered into Marlissa's ear. "You've never prepared for this many before."

"We will feed them until there is not a single inch of room left in their bloating stomachs, understood? You leave the rest to me."

After the last of supper, there was much reveling and decadence into the midnight hours. Marlissa enjoyed the company of her guests as much as possible, purposely kissing and getting her hands on as many of them as possible.

"Everyone will stay here tonight," she insisted as her visitors fell asleep one by one, passing out in intimate poses and positions.

Even those that had planned to leave by nightfall had fallen into the indulgence, passing out in the main rooms of uncomfortable furniture and carpet floor. And once the final guest had drifted off into an exhausted slumber, Marlissa moved about gracefully.

Crafting an artform that she had perfected her entire life, she decorated the manor in a very particular fashion, both inside and out. By morning's light, her forever-distracted quests would have no choice but to be captivated by her creation.

From their upstairs chambers, the male cooks locked their bedroom doors and said their holy prayers, hoping to sleep through the events downstairs.

"It's unmistakable! Come and see!"

"Why, it's a miracle... I've never even read about anything like this before!"

With the morning sun, the first to rise saw such a sight. Here, in the middle of summer, was an improbable cover of snow coating the estate's grounds. Marlissa was nowhere to be seen, as the commotion awoke the others little by little. While some joined together at the window, others sat where they woke with their hands at their stomachs, some form of a great illness apparently shared across the group.

"I don't feel so well..."

"I don't either! Was it something we ate last night?"

A few curious risers grabbed a book and ran out briskly into the ground of snow, falling and rolling, marveling and trying to throw balls of it at one another.

But something wasn't right with it, it wasn't anything close to snow.

The sick inside felt worse as their senses failed altogether, their bodies feeling soft and their sentences beginning to slur into one long word.

LAST FAKE HAPPY WORLD

The Lady Marlissa descended into her domain by a single silk thread. She still wore her powdered wig, but it was slightly pushed back, revealing additional eyes. Where her massive dress had been, now her exposed legs were shown, the thin eight black legs of her true spider nature.

The guests outside, and a few more that now tried to escape, were trapped and tangled in the sheet-web 'snow' of the domain's grounds. One by one their time would come, and the beautiful creature Marlissa would show them a true indulgence.

Those that remained inside fell into a softening panic. Their bodies liquified before their crying eyes, pre-digesting from saliva of the prior night's debauchery and what had been cooked into their dinner.

By the end of the day, Lady Marlissa slept satisfied in her lair. Those she had once entertained had outstayed their collective welcome, but there would always be more. More of the weak willed, more of the soft skinned. More of this distracted and self-absorbed human insect, incapable of seeing when a spider was playing with her food.

LAST FAKE HAPPY WORLD

Away From It All

"It says in here that people go missing at these national parks every year."

"Stop reading that stuff, Wendy, it'll mess with you. You'll get all scared, then you won't even want to leave the cabin!"

Wendy rolled her eyes and stretched. The old mattress was so stiff, but it didn't matter to her in the slightest. This was their honeymoon to America. Newlywed Niles and Wendy Walker, it had a beautiful ring to it and Wendy looked up lovingly from her book and to her husband.

"What?" he asked, sharing the sideways glance as he lay there beside her. "What's that look for?"

"Guess what?"

"Tell me," he said with increasing interest, rolling on his side to face her.

"It says that _hundreds_ of people go missing each year."

"Oh, come on, would you stop with this weird book already??"

"No, really! It's creepy!" she went on. "Where do they go? They just vanish, and the government doesn't even keep official records on it!"

"They probably fall off cliffs, or get eaten by bears, or... I don't know."

"Maybe Bigfoot? You think it's a Sasquatch? Or do you think they get 'spirited away?' Did I ever tell you about that?"

"Here we go..." Niles sighed. "You're really cute, you know that?"

Wendy stuck out her tongue jokingly and closed the book. It was their first night at the cabin and they would be up by sunrise, not to mention Niles was starting to have that telltale gleam in his eyes.

"I can tell what you're thinking," Wendy analyzed him with a seductive look.

Niles said nothing in return, meeting his bride with an embrace and feeding their healthy desires. Their passion played into the late hours of night, isolated within their private cabin in the woods.

From sunrise to sunset, the following few days were perfect and the same. They would rise with the sun, wipe the sleep from their eyes and hike out into the deep forest. Each day they explored new trails, saw new sights and took photos of the flowers, insects and waterfall streams that they came across. This was the picturesque honeymoon and away-from-it-all vacation that they had both long been waiting for.

Everything was perfect, but something was out of place.

Maybe it wasn't happening at first, or perhaps she just didn't notice, but Wendy began to see a small difference in her husband as the week went on. He was still energetic, but a step or two behind. He was still focused on exploring, but his mind seemed aloof. And at night, when he initiated the lovemaking, so soon his stamina was completely depleted.

"Going out for a walk and a smoke," Niles told her, succumbing to the nasty cigarette habit he had picked up as a teenager.

"Don't forget to come back," Wendy joked, her nose back in the book as he headed out.

His habit... While he had promised her that he would quit smoking the day after they got married, here they were on their honeymoon and already he had forgotten. Wendy didn't care much, or at least not enough to start complaining already. The last thing she wanted was to start nagging so soon after their vows.

"At least he's out walking," she said to herself, trying to fill the empty and silent cabin with the sound of a human voice.

She tried not to worry, trying not to think about the bears and wild pigs that lurked after nightfall. Instead, she read on, reading horrible examples of entire families who had gone missing in these parks.

It didn't seem so interesting tonight.

"Honey, I'm home," Niles announced a short bit later, walking

LAST FAKE HAPPY WORLD

through the door with almost a skip in his step.

Wendy still couldn't put her finger on it, but something was off kilter.

"Done with your book already?" he asked, hanging his thin jacket up on a wall peg.

Wendy was sitting in a cabin chair, the book closed at her nightgown-laced lap with a look of relief across her young face.

"You were gone a while," she told him with concern in her tone. "I was getting worried about you."

"No... Don't be worried, love!" he came to her and took the book from her lap, setting it to the side. "We're miles away from trouble out here. Nothing to worry about."

She rose to her feet and kissed him, mouth to mouth and her breath tasted his. For a change, he didn't taste like the lingering residue of tobacco smoke. In fact, his breath tasted strangely clean.

All thoughts and worries erased from her mind as they went to the bed together. Into the night, again, they made love. And just as before, again his energy was decreasing.

"Have you been feeling ok?" Wendy asked him, early to rise and pulling her long brown hair into a ponytail.

"Never felt better," he shot back with a smile to reassure her.

"You're sure that you're not catching a cold or anything?"

"No, darling," he kissed her atop her head, throwing on his baseball cap and the pair heading out into the forest again.

They hiked like they had been hiking all week, Wendy taking digital photos of regional birds and butterflies, colored leaves and the morning sun glistening through spiderwebs. New subjects she began photographing were the facial shape designs they found in rocks and trees along the way. More often than not, they disagreed on what the other saw, talking like children imagining animal shapes in the clouds.

The day flew by just as the others before, and so soon they found

LAST FAKE HAPPY WORLD

themselves back at their secluded cabin. Wendy scrolled through her photos of the day, deleting some and keeping most. Niles walked past her and grabbed his cigarette pack from the dresser near the bed.

"You're going back out?" Wendy asked and then immediately felt bad, the nagging personality shift weighing heavy in her head.

"Yesss," Niles playfully returned, dragging the sound out like a hissing snake. "Just a quick walk and smoke, I won't be long."

"Where do you even go? It's pitch black out there."

"You worry too much. Are you worried I'm going to run into the Abominable Snowman, or something?"

Wendy shook her head in disbelief. "It's called Sasquatch. Bigfoot."

"Well, fortunately for you, I've had zero sightings on the cryptozoology front. If you must know, there's a really old tree I've been checking out. See? Exciting."

Wendy went back to her photos and let her husband go out on his habitual smoke walk. The beginning feelings of abandonment crept in and Wendy shot them down immediately. Instead, she refocused her attention on the photographs, pouring over them and admiring her amateur skills. Faces in boulders, facial features in trees, one even had branches like two arms reaching out. It was almost scary in a small way and she stopped, scrolling back to the butterflies and insects.

"Honey, I'm home," came the voice of her husband, the same as the previous night only much later this time.

Wendy was already in bed and beneath the covers. She lay still, facing away from the doorway with her eyes wide open and awake, pretending to be asleep as Niles quietly went about the cabin. He had been gone so long this time that she had given up on waiting.

He slipped into bed slowly and draped his arm over her side. A slight peck of a kiss at her hair, and at last she spoke.

"Why were you gone so long?" she asked, still facing away from him.

He waited a moment before he replied. "Was I? It was about the same as last time, wasn't it?"

Wendy rolled over to face him with a frown. Their eyes met in the dark and small kisses turned into passion, though initiated by her. It wasn't long before she tried to advance the foreplay towards intercourse.

"Do you love me?" she asked with a whisper, breathing hard to match the rhythm of her heartbeat.

"Mm-hmm," he murmured and nothing more, laying there with his eyes closed and a satisfied grin on his lips.

Wendy continued, using all the methods that a new bride would use. This wasn't like the prior nights where his stamina was depleted, this was something worse. No matter what she did, no matter what dirty tricks she used on him, her husband's body was simply not responding. Like a challenge, she kept at it. Still though, only the smallest reaction.

"Am I doing something wrong?" she nervously asked, raising her head to look at him. "Niles?"

Not only was his body unreceptive to her touch, but somewhere during her attempts to arouse him, Niles had already fallen asleep.

Wendy slid back to her lonely place in the bed, laying her unfulfilled body in defeat beside her husband. Though she tried to not take it personally, her heart sank into her stomach. Maybe he was just exhausted from the hiking, and maybe she was exhausted too. Her thoughts didn't linger for long, as soon her mind began drifting off to sleep.

The last thoughts she had were the curious wonderings of why his breath had tasted so fresh again. Was he really smoking? And if not, where was he going and what was he doing?

The morning came quickly, and Wendy was soon awake and ready to go. Their honeymoon trip was winding down, and where was Niles, but still in the bed. She tried to let him rest a bit longer, cleaning up their vacationing clutter, applying a small amount of makeup that he probably wouldn't notice, and drinking more cups of coffee than she probably had all week.

She checked his cigarettes to see if he had in fact been smoking. The opened pack was nearly empty, so he had to be. She still wondered what was really going on with him, or if she had been just overly analyzing things again.

Niles was finally up, and she pushed her frantic concerns to the back of her mind. The day drifted by just as quickly as the others, hiking and photos, new sights seen and random conversations. When Wendy asked Niles about the tree he was walking to each night, he was vague, telling her it was really nothing special. When she pressed the issue, saying that she wanted to see it before the day was over, he told her that it was in completely the opposite direction.

Wendy felt the same defeat as she had in the bedroom. He was exhausted, he was evasive in communication and his mind was preoccupied with something, or someone. It brought her back mentally to a boyfriend she had long ago, Niles now showing the same signs of a man that had been cheating on her.

But out here? In the middle of nowhere? There wasn't a town around in walking distance, nor had they seen a single person since they arrived at the cabin.

Wendy put her nervous energy to work in her photography, taking more pictures of all the strange face-like things they saw in the trees and rocks. Still though, her mind couldn't help but wonder.

"I promise, I won't be so long this time. Really!"

"Can't you just stay here tonight, with me?" Wendy pleaded and nearly begged, sounding pathetic to herself. "Our trip's almost over!"

LAST FAKE HAPPY WORLD

"I'll be here with you tonight, Wendy. Just as soon as I go to have a smoke."

"Then maybe you can just stay on the porch? Don't go for a walk tonight?"

"What's going on with you lately?" he asked her with disbelief. "You've been acting a little odd these last few days. Maybe you need to rest, maybe we've been trying to do too much this week?"

Wendy let his words sink in. She had no idea what was going on with her husband or herself, and maybe she had been acting odd. She didn't dare tell him of the abnormal jealousy she was feeling today, nor of the concerns of their sexual encounter the previous night.

"Maybe I should just go to sleep then," she gave in, feeling disappointed in herself for this behavior. "I'm sorry, I'm just exhausted."

Niles smirked and wasted no time, taking up his cigarettes and a second pack, grabbing his jacket as if in a rush.

"I won't be long, just get some rest and before you know it, I'll be sleeping here beside you."

He kissed her and was already off, seeming more excited and enthusiastic than he had displayed all day. It irked Wendy and only served to stir the pot.

She grabbed her own jacket and snuck through the doorway, silently trailing her husband from afar.

Wendy thought that she should feel bad about this, but instead she felt bad that she didn't. It wasn't difficult to follow him, the noise he created was obnoxious enough to mask any distant sound she made in her pursuit. He was only walking and smoking, so far everything was as it should be. The further they traveled, the worse she felt. How would she explain it if he found her shadowing him through the woods? For that matter, she hoped she could even find her way back, that was something she hadn't considered.

LAST FAKE HAPPY WORLD

Shortly thereafter, Wendy realized that they weren't even on a trail anymore. This had turned out to be such a bad idea. It crossed her mind to call out to him now, so that she could feel safe out here beside him. Or to maybe just turn back already, they were still only a few minutes away from the cabin.
But something stopped her from doing either.
Niles had halted in his tracks. At first, Wendy began to panic, ducking down and believing he had either heard or seen her. But it wasn't that, he never turned to look. Instead, he stood there in the moonlight, facing away, and began to take his jacket off. What was this?
Soon, it was more than the jacket. He removed his baseball cap. He removed his shirt. He removed his shoes and his pants. Wendy was in complete shock as he removed his underclothing and stood there stark naked beneath the sky. Before she could even begin to comprehend what she was witnessing, he was off and walking again, completely naked in the woods.
Wendy's heart beat hard, her newlywed husband passing in full exposure between the trees. She followed even more cautiously now, soon passing his pile of discarded clothing. His ghost-like white body continued a few long strides more and then soon came to a stop.
He hadn't been lying, there was a tree he was visiting after all. It stood towering in the forest, Niles standing naked in its moonlight shadow. It was quite different than the others around it, looking unnatural, supernatural even, and Wendy observed from a safe distance as the scene unfolded.
Her husband touched it, setting his hands on the tree's bark as if meeting a lover, then climbing onto it like an animal. Wendy watched the odd situation as her nude husband began to scale the giant tree trunk. It was unsettling to see and nonsensical. In her curiosity, she took short steps closer, her eyes playing tricks on her as she looked up into the canopy and branches high above.
There was no way, and it couldn't be what it looked like, could

it? The moonlight and the dark of night blurred with sight and reality. The tree that her husband clung to looked more and more like a giant carved woman the more that Wendy's eyes followed it up. It slowly stirred and was animated like a massive dryad, Niles climbing to where the trunk became hips, up to where a thick wooden waist became full wooden breasts. And there he stood atop them, face to face with the giant woman of the tree.

Wendy's heart raced so fast now that her body was trembling. Suddenly a nighttime wind blew as vine-like branches grabbed for her arms and legs. They attached and instantly scoured her body like tentacles, wiggling in beneath her clothing and around her panting mouth. Her wrists were bound and her legs spread, her screams for Niles lost to the stems feeling inside of her mouth.

Her held-open eyes watched him as the branches lifted her into the air. He was exhaling into the dryad's mouth, who then exhaled back into his. It was a scene of perverse betrayal as Wendy was carried past, the sex organ of her husband fully erect with excitement at the exhalation exchange.

The branches strangled Wendy like a noose, sapping the blood and water from her body, absorbing and draining her entire essence like bloodthirsty roots. Her identity was vanishing as she watched her newlywed husband, pressing his pale body erotically against the unnaturally-natural form.

It gradually didn't feel wrong.
A natural purification.
Growing together, nothing needing explanation.

Time went by, and the world never saw Niles or Wendy Walker again. Their belongings were discovered in the cabin, some clothes were uncovered in the forest, but no remains were ever found.

In the years to come, as new visitors passed through the tranquil

LAST FAKE HAPPY WORLD

world of the national park, two new faces were seen within the odd shapes of an old tree in the forest. At one with nature and wildly spirited away from it all.

Don't Look Now

Today was the day I had been waiting my entire life for. Up until now, everything I had ever seen, I saw with blank-stare eyes. I had spent every single day of my life living blind, looking out into this empty shroud and searching through the black.

My brother, Helmut, had been my only guide to the world around us. To say 'brother' might be a stretch, because in essence we were the same. Two heads attached to a single body, and though granted the gift of sight, Helmut had always been the weaker of our simultaneous and shared existence.

I controlled what we did with my limb control, while he alone directed me and basked in the wonderful things we witnessed. His vanilla descriptions shared only the smallest details, though still I clung in desperation to his every word, dreaming of a day when I too could see these sights in an optical wonderland.

"Herman," his mother's nasal-drip voice called to him like a sweet song, "today's your special day, everyone is here to see you!"

And today, on this vital day of life, Herman would finally be able to see them as well.

Voices rose and shared the choir of celebration. There was the tenor voice of his uncle, high-pitched young cousins and various family friends. They shared conversations and congratulated him, though in a way it was an odd sort of thing to be congratulated for.

All that he had done was outlive his second head. Poor, deathly Helmut, with his blasted perfect sight. Curse him and his flawless functioning eyes, curse his vision that should have been Herman's in another lifetime. But now, things would be different.

Along with the successful amputation of the dead head, the doctors at the hospital had attempted an experimental surgery. An unparalleled transplant from the eye sockets of one head and to the

LAST FAKE HAPPY WORLD

other. Beneath his surgical head dressing, Herman was now in possession of the operational eyes.

The doctors had already explained the low chance of success. They had gone over the procedure and even the unlikelihood that this would ever be tried again. Herman had listened to these speeches both before and after going under the knife, nothing they could say dissuading him from the dream of seeing the beautiful world.

"It's fitting that it's your birthday today, Herman," his mother celebrated, a warm hand on his shoulder. "Even though we mourn the loss of our beloved Helmut, we still have you and after today you'll be stronger than ever. You'll finally be able to live the life of a normal boy! You'll be able to do anything you want in this world!"

There were tears in her voice, a collective sigh from the gathered company as well. Herman himself would have cried tears of joy if Helmut's eyes, now his eyes, weren't so sore beneath these bandages. Just the thought of his dead brother brought back feelings of old jealousy and resentment. But now he would have the last laugh.

"Are you ready, young man?" the voice of his doctor came from alongside him. "Give me the word and we'll remove the dressing."

"Do it, I'm ready!"

"Now, before we do," the doctor prepared everyone, "let's not forget that this was a new and experimental transplant. There's no guarantee here."

Herman gripped the armrests of his chair with glee. The doctor's callous hands worked on the wrappings, unwinding the cloth and gauze from around his remaining head. Light filtered in with each unwind, shining like a sunrise in his life. The brightness grew more vibrant, the air feeling fresh on his exposed skin. This was it, moments away from his only dream coming true. Bright lights growing brighter and lighter, blinding him with the anticipation of the approaching sights he had never seen before.

LAST FAKE HAPPY WORLD

The surgical wrappings were off. His eyes blinked, seeing only an all-surrounding light at first. Slowly and clearly it was converging into a focal point, details falling into place like small raindrops before a storm.

The gathering of family and friends stood in a silent wait. A lapse in time as Herman squinted with his jaw hanging open.

"Herman?" his mom's voice asked. "Herman, sweetheart? Can you see me? Can you see me, baby?"

Herman could see, at first foggy and then fuzzy, blinking over and over to make sure that this was right. This... This was the world, the beautiful world he couldn't wait to see?

"Mom..." he slowly said, dragging the word out as he strangely gaped at the woman before him. "Mom, is that you??"

"My baby!" she squealed and grabbed onto him, hugging his body as if meeting for the first time.

The collected mass of people cheered, but something was horribly wrong. Herman was seeing, a true joy and miraculous event, but what he now saw for the first time was nothing he imagined. Nothing in the descriptions Helmut had given him, nothing in his dreams, and nothing in his worst fears could prepare him for what he saw with perfect sight now.

"Herman, baby! Look at me! Look at your momma!"

She leaned back from the embrace, still holding him. She was hideous with ready-to-burst boils and bumps, red warts and broken skin. There was running fluid and crusty flakes at her nose, a crooked neck and patches of hair on her oddly deformed head.

Herman tried not to cringe, pulling away instinctively from the creature that was calling him son. Was this 'seeing?' Was this the gift of sight he had spent his lifetime longing for??

"Now, learning to adapt to your vision will be an undertaking," the doctor's voice explained, "but I have faith you'll take to this new miracle in no time at all. Tell me, what is it like to see for the very first time? Do you see colors explode before you, or is it dim with a grainy texture?"

Herman looked from his mother's holding arms and saw the doctor approach. There were track-like stitches and cracks across his leather-bound face, oils and pus oozing from his pores.

"You're... the doctor that operated on me?" Herman asked with a grossed-out fear shaking in his voice.

"With these very hands, my boy!"

He held out swollen claws, infected nailbeds and scabs spread across his fingers. As Herman looked closer, he saw that the arm hairs on the doctor's forearms wriggled, moving independently like tiny black worms.

"What's wrong, baby?" his mother asked as he pressed harder away from her hug. "I know it's a lot to take in, but calm down, baby. Momma's here."

Herman looked around the room in terror, his body quivering at the nightmare surrounding him. It wasn't just his mother or the doctor, all of these gathered creatures before him were like nothing he imagined. Horns and scales, shedding fur and bloated stomach bruises. They had snouts and whiskers, bent tails and wore clothes sewn from patchwork skin.

"Herman, you're turning pale!" his mother blurted out from her canker-sore lips in concern. "Can someone get him something to drink?"

Herman's eyes darted in panic, his heart off to the races. One of the gathered creatures opened a dirt-covered refrigerator.

"What does he like? Does he normally drink milk?"

The voices blended as he saw the contents of the fridge, moldy frozen walls of dark greens and browns, the shelves holding animal heads, legs and embryo-exposed eggs.

"I don't think I..." Herman tried to say, walking backwards and away from the shock of these revelations. "I have to go. I have to, I have to leave..."

His family looked confused at his poor reaction to it all, Herman

LAST FAKE HAPPY WORLD

feeling more than confused at this reality himself. Though Helmut had described things to him in the most unpoetic of ways, nothing in his dull details had ever hinted at this horror.
"Maybe he should rest for a bit?" came a voice from the pack.
"I'm fine, really I'm fine," Herman said and repeated to himself, walking by instinct through the house he had blindly lived in.
And even this house, how could he have been living like this? There was mildew on the walls, leaking bile stains at the ceiling and garbage laying everywhere. There were clumps of hair and piles of dead mice, bugs and web-covered mousetraps littering every corner.

He made his way to the front door, surely the outside world had to be more beautiful than this.

"Herman!" the doctor shouted. "Where are you going? You really should stay inside the first few days! It's a big adjustment!"
But no matter, Herman rushed through the door like a prisoner into freedom. The whole wide world was open to him now, and his ugly house and unattractive family couldn't keep him from it any longer.
Stepping out into the familiar warmth of sunlight, the added visons overwhelmed Herman in a flash.

No. It couldn't be…

As horrifying as the first sights of his family and house had been, nothing could prepare him for the outside real world. He walked out into it as if in doubt, looking over everything with his insides sinking inside. This was the world? These were the streets he traveled every day, his brother Helmut hiding it from him and saying nothing of the sort?
"Herman, you get back inside this house, young man," his mom yelled to him from the doorway behind. "I know how excited you

are, but you really need to pace yourself!"

Herman ignored her. This had to be an illusion, the world couldn't be this bad. He started walking and then jogged, heading out into the world by means of his nightmare street, terrible monstrosities abound.

The sky, how could anyone in the world accomplish anything with this abhorred sky above? It was deep purple with spots of blotting red, organ-tissue clouds and decaying birds hovering in the humid air.

A car horn blared as he stood in the road with wonder. His eyes came back down from the foul sky and stared at the menacing vehicle, living eyes for headlights and drooling fangs in its grill. An angry monster of a man yelled from behind the wheel, the hungry living car inching toward him with a devouring intent.

It absolutely baffled Herman how he could have lived in such a place and never even known about it. He began to wonder if his brother had intentionally hidden all of these realities from him, then looking to his left to see where Helmut's head would have sprung. Loose black-stained bandages flapped in the breeze, a glimpse of the rotten flesh beneath.

The car horn blasted again, its predator grill a foot away from consuming him. "Get out of the road, you freak!" the twisted driver yelled from the window, one of his eyeballs sagging from its hole.

'Freak.' Herman let the word process as he moved to the sidewalk. How was he a freak in this mad world? He ignored the thought and began to jog further away from home, seeing demolished cars left in front yards, mangled bodies torn apart and tangled in the wrecks.

Familiar voices called to him from behind, but he didn't stop. Herman's jog became a run, dashing past white worms the size of snakes. Intestinal trees gleamed in the clammy light and a pack of six-eyed dogs ran by, a humanoid-looking offspring limp within one's jaws.

LAST FAKE HAPPY WORLD

Away from the suburbs and into the muted lights of the city he entered, the begotten horrors piling up as well as bodies in the streets. There were more people like monsters here, women with faces covered in smeared clown makeup, men with tendril and pubic facial hair. White slime dripped from bloodshot eyes, orange discharge seeped from ears. There were different body types of every horrible fashion. Heavy beings with countless rolls pulling from their bodies, alongside literal skin-and-bones people with rotten black and yellow spines exposed.

Herman looked away from this grotesqueness of individuality, looking to the city itself and only seeing things much worse. People jumped from skyscrapers, burning airplanes crashed into the horizon. Multi-lane streets were littered with dead animals, the bodies scraped up like delicacies by families checkered in filth.

Thunder struck as a vein of lightning crashed from the sky. Red rain then poured from the organ-tissue clouds, covering the horrid scene in a bath of clotting plasma.

Herman's eyes throbbed from his swollen tear-ducts, ducking into an alley to escape the bleeding downpour. He couldn't live like this, what was wrong with this world?? Down the dark alley and still the blood fell, splashing on the scenes of seedy horror that existed back here. A festering beast of a woman was breast-feeding her armful of spawn, their raw tongues whipping and tentacle fingers feeling. Herman turned so he wouldn't see, instead seeing flea-bitten creatures eating from the same dumpsters that they defecated in. There was nowhere left to turn. This was a world of filth and disgust. There was no other option, he needed to escape this handicapping prison of sight.

In the crimson downpour, he clawed at his new eyes, scraping his dream-come-true nightmare until they bled and were carved to never see again. The pain was insurmountable, but the exchange well worth the cost. These things he had once been oblivious to, he needed to scratch from his mind.

LAST FAKE HAPPY WORLD

It was funny in a way, he thought as he sat there in the terrible alley. He thought about the various things he had heard throughout his life, and maybe he was wrong, but perhaps Helmut had been telling him all along. Expressions his brother had said, meaning nothing and thrown away. Things like 'spill your guts' and 'what's eating you.' How could he not have listened? Phrases like 'it grows on you' and 'keep an eye out.'

Herman laughed now, sitting in the blood.

The world had been crazy all along. Or maybe not, maybe he was the one who just didn't understand. A sigh of defeat turned into a sigh of relief.

Two heads were better than one after all. Existing out here on his own, alone, in this disgusting human city without the truth shielded or filtered. Who would want to live like this? Who could even do it?

With his new eyes now as obsolete as his old eyes, the red rain fell. In blindness, it was the same refreshing rain again, just cold water on his flesh.

Herman had made his choice. In this world, if he wanted to find true happiness, he would discover it in the comforting return to his blinding blackness. To see exactly what he wanted to see, to see precisely what he was looking for, he quite literally had to do something that his brother had once said to him.

"Herman, if somehow you ever learn to see, do yourself a favor and keep your eyes peeled."

Occult Pride

"Sorry, kid," a man at the gas station had told him years ago, "but you're wasting your time. You're never gonna find anything out there, at least not what you're looking for."

And to an extent, he had turned out to be right. Shawn had spent years searching for offbeat things, everything from hauntings to legends, from myths to mysteries and everything in between. But something about the rumored 'disappearing house' in the forests of Midlothian had stuck with him forever. When he was in grade school, he had heard classmates reciting legends about those woods across town. In high school, he had gone there with a pack of friends, fooling around and nothing seen. And as a young adult, he had ventured there alone. Aside from a few nervous scares, again the search turned up empty.

The gas station attendant had unfortunately been telling the truth. Most people explored this forest preserve with the hopes of not finding the house, but a cheap supernatural thrill. And for that, there was plenty. A plethora of ghost lore hung over this patch of trees, mostly stemming from a graveyard held nearly forgotten in the underbrush.

But the house legend was what pulled Shawn in, from grade school until now, in his late thirties. There was supposedly a house that people saw, resting out of place in the woods. It would appear once in a lifetime and then be gone, vanishing before you could reach it. But if you made it to this never-there house, and opened the door before it left, then you would go away with it.

But what would happen next? That's where the legend got off track. Some said you would simply die, others saying you would go to another dimension with it, trapped within with its ghosts. Shawn's favorite was a wild theory that if you made it inside, it would be completely empty – But once in a lifetime, there would be a man inside. There was nothing unusual about him, but once in

LAST FAKE HAPPY WORLD

a lifetime, again, there would be a key inside his pocket. If he gave it to you, you would find that it was merely a plain old key.

But then the final 'once in a lifetime.' It could be a key that opened a secret door, inside holding all the secrets of the universe.

How he would get out of the house before it vanished was an entirely different question, let alone where in the world that door would even be. But the hunt, the obsession, was the fruitless thrill that Shawn fed upon. "You're wasting your time" was both true and untrue, with unfortunately more days being true than others.

But today was peculiar. Shawn was used to coming across legend trippers, sightseers, teenage punks or sometimes random goth kids on these wishful excursions. But there was something off and completely out of place about his latest encounter.

Women could be beautiful with shaved heads, but it wasn't a sight he saw too often. His mother had gone through chemo before and lost her hair, but even then, she wore a wig. Yet here before him stood not one, but two attractive women with no hair. Both with the same black ebony skin that he had, and both standing so close to him that he couldn't help but feel uneasy.

"We've never seen you here before," one of the ladies told him, deep brown eyes sizing him up. "What are you doing here, so late at night?"

"I, I..." Shawn stammered and stuttered. "You're really not allowed to be in here after sunset... But, I... I'm doing research."

"Research?" the other woman chimed in, slowly circling him as if he were their prey. "Researching what, exactly?"

Though typically quite comfortable around women, this was all catching him off guard. Both were so unnaturally beautiful with their smooth skin heads and sleek eyes, dressing in matching cream-colored robes that fit the curves of their tall bodies.

"It's, well, you know," Shawn tried to regain composure, "these woods. There's a lot of attention here, a lot of paranormal activity here..."

"We know these woods very well," the first woman told him.

LAST FAKE HAPPY WORLD

"But what specifically are you looking for?"

Trying to focus on the reason he was even here, Shawn felt a hint of embarrassment around these two athletic, model-like beauties.

"Just ghosts... Supernatural type hauntings, things like that."

"Ah, I see," said the second woman. "Well, we wish you good luck with that, ghost hunter."

She turned to walk away, the other lingering for a moment and then turning to follow her off into the night. Shawn stayed back for a second and watched them, wondering where on earth they had even come from in the first place. He had been going to bars and nightclubs in the city, never once seeing anyone as attractive as the pair. With his 'research' put to the back of his mind, he quickly followed, wondering where they had come from and where they were now headed.

"So, um, where were you guys going?"

"*Guys?*" one of the two asked, looking over her shoulder without surprise that he was following.

"Girls, ladies," he corrected. "Were you looking for ghosts too?"

"You could say we were looking for something more substantial than that," the other added. "Something more like a house than a ghost."

"Whoa, what?" Shawn stopped in his tracks and then quickly picked up his pace to keep up. "No way! You're looking for the disappearing house too?? I've been coming here my entire life looking for that! I can't believe this, this is awesome! Do you-"

"Shhh," the closest lady put a finger to her lips. "Don't be so excited, it's just a house."

"Just a house?" Shawn repeated and couldn't help but let out a small laugh. "No offense, but it's way more than just a house. I can't believe that both of us, I mean all three of us, are looking for it! Nobody even talks about it anymore, they only talk about the ghost stuff. Which, if you ask me -"

"There's more than three of us, silly man," the woman leading the way informed him. "You aren't very alert in the darkness, are you?"

LAST FAKE HAPPY WORLD

Shawn slowed his steps but kept up, looking around in the night woods. At first, he didn't see, but shortly thereafter three more women joined the walking group. Each of them with the same shaved heads and smooth black skin, wearing the same style of the body-clinging robe.

"I... don't really understand this," Shawn's laugh felt uneasy now.

"Relax," one of the newcomers calmed him, coming up from behind with her long fingernails resting on his back. "You don't have to understand. Today is your lucky day."

"This man is looking for the disappearing house, sisters," the lead walker explained to the new arrivals. "Isn't that quite the coincidence?"

Shawn didn't know how to react, feeling herded along now by the surrounding beautiful women. In one regard, it was exciting to meet five gorgeous women alone in the woods. At the same time, the identical no-hair haircut and matching clothing made him fearful. Was it a cult? A group of Devil-worshippers?

"I lied to you," the first woman then openly admitted. "We aren't really looking for the house."

"Um, ok?" Shawn felt his nervousness rise, his fears increasing.

"Does someone want to tell him?" she threw the question back to any of the four.

"Because we already know where it is," one said in a quiet voice beside him. "Do you want to see it?"

Shawn felt dumbfounded. He had spent entire days of his life searching for this urban legend house, there was no way that they could actually know where it was – If it was even real in the first place.

"So, is it just like an old run-down house then?" he asked, trying not to be weirded out by his escorts. "The story I heard was that it disappears and reappears."

"Don't ask so many questions," one of the group replied. "You'll see for yourself when we get there."

LAST FAKE HAPPY WORLD

"Listen to her," another added before Shawn could even respond. "If you've been searching for it your entire life, just appreciate what we're doing for you then."

"And in turn," a third spoke up, "once we show you what you are looking for, you can show us what we've been looking for."

Shawn kept quiet and felt an odd mix of anxiety and hormones. He wasn't sure if they were going to make out with him or kill him, hoping he would at least get to see the old house first. He followed alongside them, through the legendary woods and toward a particular direction.

~ Something gleamed ahead in the distance ~

Before he could speak, the leading woman gave him a knowing look, silencing his voice. There was a house there, through the trees and almost glowing in the night. Impossible. It was dark, but he knew this small forest well enough to know that there was no house here before.

The 'disappearing house.' Was it real now?

It looked old and abandoned, yet for some reason felt new and inviting.

He attempted to run toward it and was instantly halted by the impossibly strong arm of the leading woman.

"It's not going anywhere," she contained him with her forceful stop. "You'll see it."

Shawn looked to the others around and they all shared the same expression. An aweless cheer, a complacent victory. The nighttime sounds of insects went quiet, all the distant noises in the world funneling away to emptiness.

"Is this actually it?? I can't believe this is happening," Shawn whispered to himself, wanting to believe it was something special.

The way it illuminated was unnatural. The closer they came, the more unusual the effect. It was like the spirit of a dead house, the soul of a home sitting silent now as a grave. There was no turning back. With or without his strange group of women, Shawn had to go in, he had to see it from the inside. If it was what he wanted it to be, who knows what would happen to him next. If it was just an elaborate hoax, he wanted in on the trick.

But this was nothing like a joke. His bones felt it as they reached the three-step stairway to the glowing door, the leading woman walking right up without hesitance.

She turned the knob and the door opened to blackness. She turned back and looked, reaching her hand out for Shawn.

He looked around to the women of the eccentric shared style, all of them heading up toward the house.

He looked to the woods, as if leaving this world and saying his goodbye.

He looked to the full moon in the starry sky, then taking the waiting hand of the woman, leading him inside.

The house interior was from another time and gothic, draped in red and black wallpaper and carpet. Candles were lit everywhere, the windows were boarded up. The women locked the door with an inside-key so that he could never escape without them.

"Kill him, or we'll kill you," one of the women growled like an animal.

They cornered Shawn in the front room, their orders of violence not directed toward him, but to a man who rested before them. In a throne chair sat a sick man, shriveled and near the end of his life. His hair and beard were long and feral, a contrast to the females' sleek and shaved appearance. Medical tubing and wires extended from his tired body, leading to unseen devices.

"You want me to do what??" Shawn asked in shock as he was forced to stand before the helpless man. "This is crazy!"

"I will repeat myself only once," the same woman ordered him to listen. "You are here for a predetermined reason. If you don't kill him now, we kill you."

LAST FAKE HAPPY WORLD

A knife was placed in his hand by the vicious stranger. She held it against his grip and her eyes bore down on him, Shawn sensing the unworldly strength in her body. To try and fight back, even with this knife, would be futile.

His eyes turned to the long-haired man. He was already near death, blood slowly rocking back and forth in the tubes attached to his skin. Shawn had never even thought about killing anyone before.

"This is stupid!" he said and turned, waiting for everyone to laugh or a camera crew to come out. "What is this, like a practical joke, a TV show or something? We can't just kill this guy!"

No laughter. The dark-skinned women just stood there, flames of ire raging in their eyes. Shawn met each of their glaring gazes and knew there was no humor. For whatever reason, he was being forced to kill this man.

He held the knife up to the man's bare chest, feeling the pulse vibrate through the cold weapon. It didn't speed up, it didn't slow down.

He pretended to try, stopping before it broke the skin.

"Show some resolve!" the nearby woman yelled and grabbed his hand, forcing him to plunge the knife into the withered heart of the dying man.

"What the hell!?" Shawn screamed and tried to pull out, the lady's amazonian strength forcing him to keep it in.

"It's the natural order of things," she calmly breathed. "He has to leave us in order for you to take his place. It's how nature designed it to be."

There was no fighting back. Every attempt that Shawn made, he was met with overpowering violence. The females were in control, forcing him to make decisions that they wanted him to make. He tried for the locked door with no luck. He tried to run away and hide in the house, but they were too quick. They escorted him to an upstairs room and showed him the inside.

LAST FAKE HAPPY WORLD

"These are not your sons," one of the women told him. "These were the offspring of the man who came before you."

Shawn said nothing, his face a mess of sweat and tears. Inside the room were five male children of a youthful age, playing with toys and simple games. Their collective attention looked up when the door opened, waving and then returning to their distractions.

"You know what you have to do," one of the five ordered him, temporarily closing the door. "It's nature's design."

"What? Are you kidding me??" Shawn tried to resist but again was grabbed, silencing him immediately.

"This is the law of a pride," she snarled. "You've killed our King Lion, now you kill off his male heirs."

"You people are insane!" Shawn pushed off and tried to escape, a fruitless endeavor yet again. "Let me out of this stupid house, you psychos!!"

Two of the women hissed, their eyes glowing like cats, their canine teeth as sharp as fangs. Shawn stepped down, terrified beyond measure.

"The house is already gone from your world. Your fate is already decided, King Lion."

"What are you talking about?? And don't call me that!"

"Listen to us right now," one of the women took charge. "Killing a man? Killing his children? That's all forbidden in your made-up human world, we know. But as soon as you stepped through that door, you left that world behind. There is no artificial law here, there are no fabricated morals. We follow our natures."

This close to her, Shawn understood that what he was dealing with wasn't human. There was something primal in her eyes, something wild and even otherworldly that he couldn't defeat. It was their way or death, or perhaps even a fate worse than death in this horrible disappearing house.

"Do it with the knife."

LAST FAKE HAPPY WORLD

Initially he couldn't, but eventually Shawn had no choice but to open the door once more. He entered in cascading tears and under the merciless guiding hands of his female captors, slaughtering the room's children until the walls ran red with their blood. It was the worst thing he could have ever imagined, beside himself with the horror he was forced into.

This nightmare was only beginning.

Downstairs once more and the ferocious women disrobed, their flawless muscular bodies standing side by side in perfection. Shawn lay at the floor in his own sorrow and the children's blood, the women advancing onto him. It was a time to reproduce they had told him, to mate and replace the fallen heirs with the offspring of his own bloodline.

He was too shattered of a man to care anymore, his body reacting only automatically when touched. They held him down and raped him, mating until pure pleasure became raw pain, his turned-on body shutting itself off from the blistering agony.

When he awoke, his view was different now. Shawn accepted what this was, something far past his realm of understanding. He was propped up in the throne chair, the medical tubes and wires now extending from his own skin, slowly draining blood and the life force from his body.

"...If you really believe that you're lions..." he fought to say, able to move his lips only in the smallest of ways. "Lionesses, or whatever... Aren't you supposed to go out and hunt..."

"We do when we need to," one of the ladies answered, Shawn's freshly drained blood stained across her mouth. "That's how we got you."

"This is our house," another walked up to his helpless body and stated, "but it's your pride land now. You can live here and rule us for as long as you can live and bleed. Your hair will grow out into a beautiful mane, you will sire beautiful heirs to your throne."

"But if your body drains or ages too rapidly in this subspace," a third added, "we'll return to your world and hunt another human to dethrone you, King Lion. To kill you, to kill your cubs and to claim your pride for his own."

"… You evil… vampire bitches…"

One of the lioness ladies ran her clawed fingernail across the growing stubble on his cheek. "This supersedes good or evil, King Lion. A male's pride is only natural."

Relive and Revenge

"You have no idea how crazy you're driving me," Victor told his girlfriend, driving down the dark highway, high-beam headlights shining in the night.

"Yeah? Then why don't you pull over for a few minutes?" Holly tempted him. "There's no one else out here."

Victor grinned but drove on, his foot hard on the gas pedal. It was a short drive back from Milwaukee to Chicago, three in the morning and the Wisconsin roads deserted.

"If you keep kissing on me like that, I'm gonna end up in the ditch."

"Just keep your eyes on the road," she told him. "I'll concentrate on what I'm doing, you concentrate on what you're doing."

Victor ignored her words and focused on the kissing instead. He always had the hottest girlfriends, and even if their shelf-life was typically three to four months, he made sure they made their stay worthwhile. Holly had been with him for a whirlwind two-month period so far, the inevitable breakup only a few good fights away.

But for now, Victor reaped the rewards of his good looks. He knew that his personality wasn't going to win him any favors. But with the right look, the right words and the right amount of spontaneity, he had somehow dated every girl that he had ever desired. This material existence was good to him, and he ran his fingers through Holly's soft hair.

"Staying at my place tonight?" he asked her, already knowing she would.

"Mm-hmm," Holly agreed.

This was the life. He looked at her lustfully for a brief matter of seconds, his eyes then peacefully returning to the blackened highway.

In a blur of shock, reaction and panic, Victor's sportscar plowed into a deer standing in the middle of the road. Those quick seconds merged into one, brakes slammed, and the steering wheel jammed clockwise, the car veering off into the gravel and grass shoulder before coming to a stop.

"Jesus! What was that?!" Holly cried, her hands spread out onto the dashboard.

"A God damn deer!" Victor pounded the steering wheel in anger. "Are you kidding me??"

He unlatched his seatbelt, quickly getting out to see the damage, more concerned for his precious automobile than Holly or the animal.

"Is it dead??" she asked, getting out as well, standing in her shorts with her hoody pulled together.

"I don't know!" Victor shouted in rage, kneeling to check the hood and bumper. "I just got this damn car too, I can't believe it. Out of all the stupid things for an animal to do! How freaking stupid can you get??"

Holly lit a cigarette and stood huddled in her hoody, the spring air warm but her body still shaking.

"I don't see it," she said as she looked around, the deer nowhere in sight. "Do you think it's alive?"

"Do I look like I give a damn?" Victor asked coldly, running his finger across a streak of blood. "It better hope that it's dead. You don't jump in front of a guy's car and get away with it. I can't believe this."

"Relax," Holly put her hands on her boyfriend's shoulder line. "It doesn't even look like there's a dent."

"You want me to relax? Why don't you just get back in the car and shut up?"

Holly bit her lip and did as told, getting back into the passenger seat with her cigarette dropped to the ground. She hated when he was like this, and now their carefree night was ruined in an instant.

The remainder of the car ride home was mostly silent, a few small words and brief exchanges here and there, but the mood had changed. Holly was more upset about the deer than being told to shut up. That she could deal with, she had dated hotheads like Victor before. But that poor animal, she thought. Helpless and probably hurt or worse, somewhere out there in the night.

There was a small, consistent rattling from somewhere beneath the car as they drove on, but neither said a word. The anger was apparent on Victor's face at the sound, his grip tightening at the wheel. They drove without stopping, into the dark while staying silent, no music on or words the short remainder of the trip.

Their lovemaking that night was without love, rougher than usual and without any of their strange fetishes. It was plain and fulfilling on a basic level, but nothing more. Victor was still furious about his car, Holly emotional about the deer. The violent passion served only as a cathartic outlet for the man, both then collapsing into an exhausted sleep by dawn.

"Can I use your car to go get cigarettes?" Holly woke her boyfriend up with a Sunday afternoon kiss. She had been up for an hour, getting dressed and putting the events of the night behind her.
"Take your car," he answered with his eyes closed, resting flat on his stomach and staying in bed.
"But it's blocked in by yours..."
Victor opened his eyes, his head still sideways at his pillow. "Then move it. And use yours."
"Ok," Holly forced a smile and headed out, grabbing both sets of keys from the kitchen counter.
Resentment was building up inside. His directness annoyed her, his reaction to the deer and more. She should've headed back to her apartment when they got home last night, she thought. But too late for that now. She would spend the day with him when she got back and see how he treated her. Then she would have to start thinking about their future.

LAST FAKE HAPPY WORLD

Into the driveway and past her small and unwashed car Holly walked, an embarrassing sight compared to his overbearing sportscar. She was surprised that he was even letting her move it after the way he had acted last night. She approached it and hoped there wasn't any blood.

The car looked to be fine, other than a few small dings visible in the sunlight. No doubt Victor would lose his mind all over again once he saw them. But then she saw something she would never be able to erase from her mind –

Holly screamed, the mangled head and pieces of the small deer were somehow jammed in the space between the car frame and its rear tire. Bloodstained fur and shredded skin clinging to the exposed bone, Holly dropped the keys and ran inside frantically.

Victor didn't take the news well, eventually calling a tow truck and having a mechanic remove the wedged remains. Holly left that Sunday night, still shaken up, and then avoided Victor's calls for several days.

It was two Saturdays later before Holly found herself back at Victor's house again. Things were sort of back to normal, there were screwed up conversations and jokes and stupid television shows. The deer scene still sat in the back of her mind, but she didn't dare bring it up at all. It was comforting to at least see her boyfriend back to his old self again, and they soon settled in for the night.

Fetish was playing a growing role in their relationship. Though it was relatively new to Holly in action, she was familiar enough with it to participate. A 'Dominatrix.' Anything less Victor would call boring. The night of the deer, he had been far too enraged to be submissive, but things were now seemingly back to their version of what was normal now.

Victor lay shirtless on the bed, wearing black latex shorts and a bondage mask. Holly then entered the room dressed as he preferred her to. Her blonde hair was slicked back into a high ponytail, her entire body covered in a red latex bodysuit. These were the lone times he allowed her to be in control. But even then, it was only by his instruction.

She twirled the braided whip like a cyclone, walking towards the bed with her spike heels tapping at the floor. Victor was hungry for the abuse, the two-week separation between them had only made the longing worse.

"You're a horrible human being," she told him with authority in her voice. "You are below a dog."

"I am."

"Silence, pig! You are lower than the underside of a snake. You are a blind maggot, buried beneath a worm."

"I beg your forgiveness, Mistress..."

"You will only speak when I – Wait a minute," Holly returned to her usual mousey voice. "Victor, what the heck is that??"

She had broken her bondage role, her eyes catching something new and out of place on her boyfriend's bedroom shelf.

"Are you freaking serious??" she drilled him before he could even answer. "Is that what I think it is??"

Victor sat there stupefied until his eyes followed her line of sight. "Oh yeah, you like it?" he unwittingly asked. "The guy at the shop asked me what I wanted to do with it once he got it out. He said he never saw one wedged in like that before."

Holly was enraged. The skull of the small deer was sitting like a bookend on his shelf, its hollow eye-holes staring out lifelessly into the bedroom.

"You just have to get that extra skin off. You boil water and -"

"No," Holly stopped him, not wanting to hear anything about it, "shut up, just shut up. I'm getting my things."

She stormed out of the bedroom, the painful sight of the roadkill skull triggering her built up animosity. For two weeks she had thought long and hard about how horrible of a person Victor was. And now, keeping that poor animal's skull as some sort of trophy was the last straw.

"Come on!" he followed her out of the bedroom. "Why are you acting so stupid? Is it your period? Is your period starting?"

"Wow," Holly laughed with an offended emotion, "you know every time I think you can't be more of a jackass, somehow you find a way to prove me wrong."

Victor pushed her from behind, knocking her down to the living room floor. She squirmed in the uncomfortable latex suit, Victor then pinning her to the floor violently.

"Don't you *ever* talk to me like that again, do you understand me??"

Holly lay helpless beneath him, a soulless rage within his eyes. This was the first time she had ever spoke up to him about anything, and this was the exact reaction she feared. His violent temper ruled him, waiting inside like a volcano. He was stronger than her and she was left with no alternative.

"Victor, I'm sorry," she forced herself to say, tears beginning to roll onto her cheeks. "I… shouldn't have... talked to you like that."

The anger in his glare didn't waver, it was a fever he was locked in and Holly was scared to death.

But from out of nowhere, there was an interrupting small crash in the other room, the sound of something falling. Victor sat still, still pinning Holly to the floor. A slight dragging sound next, followed by a loud impact that startled them both. The smash of something thudding against the wall.

In an instant, the abusive struggle was paused, Victor coming to his feet and standing over his girlfriend.

"Is someone in here??" she asked him in trembling words.

He raised a finger to his unzipped mask lips, motioning for her to stay silent. Holly sat up, too scared to react and watched as her boyfriend walked softly to the bedroom.

Disappearing through the doorway, and then a yell came from deep within his throat. It was an alarming sound of fear that Holly had never imagined hearing from him, followed by the continuous sounds of things toppling over. Before she could even gather her thoughts, his body was thrown back out of the room, hitting the adjacent wall and then falling to the floor.

"Victor!" Holly screamed, standing now with weak knees.

He looked to her and acted as if he was about to say something, but instead his sight returned to the bedroom's open door.

Out from it rushed a terrifying sight. It was the skull of the deer, levitating in midair and surrounded by an apparition body of its once-living self. It jumped high and kicked, bucking and running through the apartment without control. Framed photos fell from the walls, bookshelves were knocked over and the television smashed.

Holly cowered against a wall screaming, Victor standing with his legs bent and arms open as if he would try to catch it. It ran by, sliding on the carpet, crashing around the kitchen and then back out again.

"What do we do??" Holly tried to scream over the wild ghost's racket of destruction. "What is it??"

"How am I supposed to know?!" Victor shouted back, the ghost deer sideswiping him again.

Holly pressed hard against the wall behind her, fearing for her life. The ghost deer acted as if in a tremendous amount of pain, all of its flailing like it was locked into the agony of its fatal highway death. Out through the door Victor scrambled, down the driveway and into the street. He was still in his latex shorts and bondage mask, his bare feet hitting the pavement as the haunted deer skull and its ghost body gave chase.

The faster he ran, the faster the ghost followed. The street was empty at this hour, no one hearing his shouts for help as he dashed past houses of complete stillness in the night. The ghost gained on him, its blue-white legs running now without the stumbling pain it had shown inside the house.

Victor looked and saw it was upon him, then dropping to a crouch position and holding his arms over his head in terror.

LAST FAKE HAPPY WORLD

The deer ghost passed through, its skull floating past as its phantom body raced on. Victor felt relief for that small instance, thinking the nightmare was finished and gone. But his masked face turned back to the road he had ran, then witnessing a supernatural sight no creature would ever wish to see.

It was the 'Wild Hunt.' The curtain of darkness had been pulled back to reveal a gathering from the spirit world in full. Horses of bone and glowing meat galloped his direction, riders with skeleton bodies and the 'Hounds of Hell' running beside them. There was a rider that blew a great horn as Victor came to his shoeless feet, slowly beginning to jog and gradually shifting into a painful run.

All thoughts escaped him, the horns and gallop of the skeleton riders behind him like a parade of death. He inadvertently followed the now distant deer as his feet blistered, running like a hunted animal, scared and lost on the road. There were no thoughts of Holly, no thoughts of his house or his expensive sportscar. Every house was dark and not a single person was awake. It was just the deer, himself and the hunt.

But he wouldn't give up. The barking grew louder, the ghostly stampede of hooves on the asphalt came closer, and Victor ran faster than he had ever run in his entire life. Down the street and he gained on the phantom deer, soon running alongside it. He looked and saw its physical skull engulfed in the transparent shroud. It moved with the spirit of a real animal, the sounds growing ever closer behind them.

His feet ached, possibly bleeding with each rapid step. A sign passed that read 'dead end,' but there was no choice. He continued running to the dead end and then through a yard. Through dark trees and he struggled, the horns blaring again behind him. So close now, but he couldn't stop. The trees grew thicker and the lights of the city fell away. Sticks and rocks underfoot cut at his feet, quickly losing speed and even faster losing hope. The deer pulled ahead now and ran as quickly as it would if it were still alive, reinvigorated by its return to the trees.

LAST FAKE HAPPY WORLD

Victor stumbled, struggling to stay on his feet to no avail. He hit the ground in a dangerous exhaustion, his chest pounding close to a heart attack. There was no escape, the horn sounded again, and he turned to face his hunters.

There were four riders at the front. The skeleton of Death's head flew with its horse above the others, blowing its hunting horn of doom. There were two skeleton riders flanking the left and right, the reaching arms of Death. And in the center of the hunting party, riding alongside the Hounds of Hell, was the final collector of life, the Grim Reaper known as Death.

Victor sat breathless as they raced toward him at full speed. His mind prayed, maybe they were after the deer, maybe they were just a nightmare or a haunting dream. They came close quickly, their empty skull faces staring out like doors into eternity.

He braced himself as they arrived and passed through, through his physical body and his inconsequential existence. He felt the ultimate pain of the end as they cut through him, hitting his soul in the same unforgiving way that his car had struck the deer. It felt forever and fatal, eternally locked in revenge-pain at this final moment.

Victor's dead face whitened beneath his mask, as if he had seen a ghost. With Death his soul left, a trophy fit for the shelves of Hell.

LAST FAKE HAPPY WORLD

To Hell With Vacation

There is an excitement that only children can feel on the night before vacation. The young imagination stretches out as they finally go to sleep, filled with thoughts of uncharted adventures and beckoning discoveries, their anticipation and ultimately the ensuing restlessness. Rolling around in bed, wondering if they'll ever fall asleep, staring at the clock as it ticks into the unknown hours.

And then at last, the dreams.

But some children have vacation dreams that are worse than others. Peter's family took vacations that would make normal children shrivel up and die. Though he had grown somewhat resilient to them by now, still the night before was difficult. And no matter what nightmare interpretation this time manifested in his over-active brain, nothing would match the terror, or thrills, that would soon be thrust upon him.

There was no one like him in the crowd here. Sure, there were other humans, but they were either dead or just in human costumes. Peter had the unique upbringing of being the sole adopted child of Mr. and Mrs. Pitchford, monsters that covertly lived on the crumbling crust of the Earth. Of course, in their everyday lives they dressed in human skin, wore human clothes, worked boring human jobs and did all of the normal and extremely pointless things that human beings would do. All monsters on the surface did that. But when the summertime came, and families across the land raced off to different tourist traps, the Pitchfords sometimes traveled to a world below the root.

The 'Black Mass Mountain' theme park.

LAST FAKE HAPPY WORLD

The infernal park of horror. As a human, Peter had no option but to stand out like a thorn with his dull tan shorts and sneakers, a baseball cap that at least had monster eyes, and his black *HellScan* shirt that unfortunately matched his parents.

All three stood in awe, gazing at the literal mouth of madness 'HellMouth' entrance way. It was a living and breathing giant face, fur covered with twisted spiral horns, its eyes watching everything like beady living cameras.

Though he had promised himself that he wouldn't, Peter couldn't help but look at the vacationers around him. Gangly monsters of every height and deformity that he could imagine. Broken horns, skin bumps and triangle tails too. They had the skin colors of a landfill, the hair colors of a swamp or sewer. His own parents fit right in, their human skins cast and shed. Both were of the same monster race, pool-blue flesh with blackish bumps, short yellow horns, thin black hair and pitch-black eyes.

Through the HellMouth entrance, and the anticipation welled up within him. Peter was finally back... He was far too young to appreciate it the last time, a few years ago, but not now. What had scared him before he now looked forward to, and what had grossed him out last time, hopefully now would only make him cringe.

The ticket-gates beyond the HellMouth had winding lines of tourists, wrapped around and waiting, lining up forward and then intersecting backwards. Fire from the park ahead illuminated their sweating shapes, a purgatory of waiting and voice chatter, all of which the Pitchford family proudly walked right past.

"Told you these HellScan shirts were the way to go, didn't I?" Mr. Pitchford proudly reminded the family, saying it loud enough to make sure others nearby could hear.

The three of them marched past the forever coiling lines, under automatic scanners that read their shirts, and out into the brilliant fire-light flames of the Black Mass Mountain.

Joy overcame them as they stood before the Hellish majesty of it,

LAST FAKE HAPPY WORLD

soaking it in with the scorching heat on their skin. The shops, the stage, the park's namesake Black Mass Mountain burning high into the underworld's cavern sky. Monsters were taking photos, holding hands and sharing in the wonder of this diabolical place.

Peter's mother handed him a park map and his eyes poured over it. The entire park design looked like a misshapen circle of a skull, dotted with killer rollercoasters and graveyards, haunted houses and boiling water rides.

"Peter, look!" his mother put her monstrous arm around him, directing his eyes back up from the map. "Look, it's starting!"

And like magic, a stage show then began, coming to undead life before them. 'The Guillotine, Gallows and Stake Show" started, a musical on the performance stage against the park's centerpiece mountain. Monsters in bright jumpsuits danced a choreographed routine, singing about a happy 'end of the world' in a way that made it feel not so bad after all.

"And now, monsters and demons of the world," a theatrical voice snarled over the music of the loudspeakers, "please welcome to the stage... The one and only, Black Mass Mouse!"

The song became happier and up-tempo as eyes set to the Black Mass Mountain. Massive, oversized black doors opened outwards, the park's ever-popular mascot stepping out onto the stage.

"Howdy, demons and devils!" the famous creature greeted. "Who's ready to lose their head?"

He was the shape and height of a cartoon man with large mouse ears. A mouse snout protruded from a draped black executioner's hood-mask, the rest of his body concealed in a skin-tight black latex. Monster children screamed and hollered, whistling and clapping as he strutted back and forth. He released the guillotines to chop heads, triggered trapdoors to let bodies hang, and lit the flames to burn bodies at the stake.

A freshly severed head rolled into the crowd and the monsters erupted with applause. Someone threw it back, the Black Mass Mouse then punting the bloody sphere like a football.

LAST FAKE HAPPY WORLD

"Come on," Mr. Pitchford suggested, "let's get to the rides while everyone's here watching!"

A great idea, and Peter couldn't help but look back as they raced away from the stage. Screams from the burning stakes and blood rolling down the latex mouse. This was a horrible place and Peter was horrified, but for some reason he loved it all the same.

There was so much to see and too much to do, the Pitchfords rushing past the shops of souvenirs for now, the roaring crowds behind in the distance. Ferris wheels loomed, black star shapes of ancient bone, riders hanging on and sometimes falling to their deaths. There was an odd train that passed, circling the park for a showcase and transportation. Its engine emitted scorching flames from a dragon-headed face, its connected cars carved out of the same dragon's body.

There was a children's activity section, full of cemetery graves and plots, young monsters sitting on tombstones as another park mascot, Graveyard Goose, entertained and told murderous stories.

Peter's mother looked to him as they rushed past, then deciding not to even ask her growing boy.

The Pitchfords arrived alongside a handful of others at the 'Servants of the Serpent' black-track roller coaster. Through the cathedral exterior and past a room of pews, here black-outfitted nuns in black featureless masks led them in groups to an altar room. Peter and his parents, alongside a handful of others, were prompted to kneel by the nuns.

It was a holy room with no expense spared, a well-crafted shrine to a horrible black snake. There was a painting behind the altar of it battling an army of human men, teeth bared and blood bleeding. Candles and stained glass adorned every wall, slithery sounds piping in and serpentine crosses hung upside down. Peter's group looked around in thrills and excitement, appreciation for the detail in this ride's holy waiting room.

"The wait is forever!" a booming voice filled the air, startling his mother and a few of the others. "But what truly is forever to we the rodents of this viper's den?"

Peter looked for the source of the voice, accidently meeting eyes with a young monster girl kneeling in the group.

"It can STRIKE without warning!" the voice shouted, catching Peter off guard as he quickly looked away. "And what are we frail things, but Servants of the Serpent..."

The source of the voice crossed into the room, standing at the altar before the kneeling guests. It was another park character, the Perdition Pig. He wore the same black latex, only on a heavier frame and with a pig nose, beneath a sacrilegious robe.

As he rambled on about the creature, Peter snuck another look at the monster girl a few guests down beside him. She was cute, for a monster, though probably a few years older than him. Her skin was a light brown, with pink hair and short blue horns, her body a quite attractively humanoid form, from what he could see.

She suddenly returned the look and his heart skipped a beat, his breath holding and his eyes struggling not to look away... She smiled like a laugh, a sweetness on her face that pierced through every ugly thing surrounding them in the room.

And then a nudge from his father broke him from her hypnotic gaze.

Everyone was staring at him, Peter feeling like he was back in school again, a student that hadn't been paying attention. His father motioned with his head toward the altar, where Perdition Pig was standing in wait.

"Well?" the pig demanded, a snort from his thick snout. "Will you or will you not shed your skin for the great serpent of below?"

"Um...." Peter thought out loud as he recovered from the uneasiness. "Yes?"

"Wonderful!" the pig declared, the theatrical mood in the small altar room returning. "Everyone now, follow this young follower's example and shed your skin for the great serpent! Go on, stand up and shed your skin! This is the end of innocence!"

Slowly and unsure the group stood up, those that were wearing clothes removing them, others peeling off additional skin layers and furs.

"Um, excuse me," Mr. Pitchford asked the robed pig as he and his wife undressed, "but these will be here when we get off the ride, right? I paid a lot of money for these HellScan shirts..."

"Throw your worries of the flesh aside, servant!" the pig grandly declared, then leaning in for a whisper. "Of course, of course... We'll have everything ready at the ride's exit, no need to worry!"

Peter felt nervous again, slowly taking off his hat and beginning to remove his shirt. He tried not to look at the cute monster girl but did so anyway, seeing her reach to remove the small top that she wore.

"Peter, fold your shorts with your underwear so they don't get lost," his mom interrupted, instantly turning his voyeurism into embarrassment. He quickly did as he was told, standing with no confidence in human nudity among these monsters.

The wall behind the altar opened, the serpent painting sliding upwards and revealing an exit out into the ride staging area, the heat from Hell drifting in.

"Go forth, Servants of the Serpent!" Perdition Pig ordered them. "Ride your faith into the venomous paradise beyond!"

The nuns ushered the group into an area where they would board the roller coaster. Peter was too ashamed and exposed to look for the girl again, instead focusing on the ride with his family, though thoughts of her persisted.

"Isn't this exciting?" his naked mother asked, standing at the edge of the waiting platform.

Peter nodded, directing his attention at the ride ahead. It was more like a highway than a typical roller coaster, a flat surface that rose high and dropped, twisting around with highwalls on all sides. His first experience here had been traumatizing, but he knew what to expect now.

LAST FAKE HAPPY WORLD

First, a giant machine drove through, full of bodies both alive and dead. At its rear were grinding gears and a buzzing saw output, shredding up the meats and bones of the flesh and blood within. This passed over the entire length of the track, leaving a trail of food for the wicked snake, a massive black scaled serpent as large as the dragon train from earlier. Its eyes and mouth were covered with a blinding harness, its back outfitted with uncomfortable seats. The black nuns escorted Peter and his group onto the living and breathing attraction.

Their arms were strapped down, their waists were strapped in and their eyes were blindfolded shut. Before the snake would be allowed to see, they would have to sacrifice their sight, and now the ride began.

Everyone cheered as the snake roller coaster took off, slithering a winding path forward through the track. No one could see as they screamed, winding up inclines and dropping even faster down, the snake rushing to swallow all of the fleshy waste that had been laid out to eat. Around and around, up and down. Jerking back and forth and feeling sick, the hot wind roasting everyone's naked bodies and heating their restraints. This ride was pure torture, and Peter hated it all throughout, but loved it so much afterwards.

Still though, throughout these wild thrills, somehow his mind kept wandering back to thoughts of the monster girl.

"So, what do you boys want to ride next?" Mrs. Pitchford asked as they walked the park, back in their HellScan shirts again.
Peter was watching to see where the girl had gone after the ride's exit, already losing track of her.
"I don't know, what about the Brickbat Mansion?" Mr. Pitchford suggested. "You like haunted houses still, don't you, Peter?"
"Yeah, yeah... We could do that, I guess."
"Well, let's head over there and see how crowded it is then," his

mother said. "Even with these shirts, they can only let so many monsters in there."

Peter walked alongside his family, taking in the sights but still secretly looking for that monster girl. They passed a skeleton carousel of electric chairs, the passengers frying and electrocuting, sweating oils and boils blistering.

"Are you having fun, dear?" his mother couldn't help but ask, noticing his distraction. "You're not too old for this sort of thing now, are you?"

"No, no, I love it," he reassured her. "I'm just taking it all in, that's all."

"I bet those human brats back at school would pass out if they saw you now, eh boy?" his father nudged him. "Imagine their faces if they saw that roller coaster??"

Peter agreed, relaxing a little, but keeping an eye out still for the girl he couldn't find.

They soon arrived at the park area of the Brickbat Mansion, 'Brickbat Boulevard.' Here, there were decorated dead trees of a simulated forest, posted warning signs of 'KEEP OUT!' and other threatening words. Barbwire was wrapped on posts and beartraps were hidden in the dead leaves of the ground, the Pitchford family cautiously making their way through.

The Mansion was ahead and a horrible attraction, one that Peter had already planned to sit out on. It was a theme park haunted house, but worse, actual torture and beatings taking place deep within. He had heard stories that they were extra cruel and abusive to humans, so there was absolutely no way he was going into the rickety haunted house.

"Are you sure?" his mother questioned him before they headed in. "You'll be fine out here by yourself?"

"He's a big boy now!" his father proudly reminded her, brushing a clawed hand against his son's face. "Besides, he could do with a break from us for a while. Wander around, get yourself something to eat. We should be back outside in an hour or two."

"Sometimes it's three," Mrs. Pitchford added.

"Meet us back here at the entrance in no more than three hours, boy. Got it?"

"Yeah, guys, sorry," Peter apologized. "It's just too much for me in there, I think..."

"Don't worry about it!" his father comforted him with a sharp smile. "You never know, maybe you'll meet a nice monster girl out here, haha!"

A nice monster girl... Peter watched his parents disappear into the torture house of the Brickbat Mansion. He was still searching the passing crowd, coming and going nobodies, still pointlessly watching for that girl from earlier.

After lingering around the Mansion's entrance for a while, Peter wandered off to escape the hideous screams and cries. Through the trees he walked while carefully avoiding the traps, his appearance looking out of place to the beasts and demons that he passed. It was so odd to him how strange things could eventually become familiar, a normal kid wouldn't even know about this secret reality, let alone be able to survive it. And here he was, so accustomed to this underworld that he was on his own, walking without fear.

Or at least in part.

Time passed, and he had eaten just a small portion of the tentacle food he ordered. Everything down here was boney or slimy or worse, sometimes even having an assembly of eyes that watched. What remained he had left for the birds in the food courtyard, brazen bat-like things that struggled for every crumb that was dropped. They fought each other and tore at the leftovers as Peter walked off, looking for something fun to pass the time.

He pulled the rolled-up map out and looked it over, looking for something safe enough that he could survive, or maybe a show that his parents wouldn't have wanted to see.

"You should try going to the Brickbat Mansion," a beautiful voice shocked him, up close and within his personal space. "It's not far from here, it's right through those trees."

It was her...

The monster girl from the roller coaster, and Peter was instantly taken aback. He could brave this horrible Hell of a theme park just fine, but girls were still a completely unknown danger to his young and nervous heart.

"I..." he trembled and struggled, unable to speak or think in the surprise.

"I'm Becky," the brown monster girl cheerfully greeted, her unnaturally bright blue eyes as striking as her brilliant pink hair. "I think you would like the Mansion, every monster does."

As she spoke, up close to him like this, it felt so incredible. It was like a friend he suddenly had, or a stranger that had instantly transformed into someone he always knew.

"I'm, I'm sorry... I can't go in," Peter weakly stated, feeling stupid and uncool as soon as he said the words.

"Why?" she shot back, her shining blue eyes unblinking.

She was standing so near him, only his parents had ever stood this close to him on purpose.

"You're so funny," she told him as he failed to respond in time, taking a small step back. "Don't you remember me? I was on the Servant of the Serpent with you."

"Of course I remember you!"

"Well, what's your name?"

"Peter, I'm Peter Pitchford," he introduced and reached to shake her hand, feeling suddenly stupid for the second time in the same minute.

Her hand was soft for a girl monster, or at least what he expected girl monster hands to feel like. In fact, she looked nothing like a monster at all. The small shorts and shirt she wore, the young girl human features only altered by the miniature blue horns at her hair, as well as odd scars he now noticed running up her arms.

"You're a weird one, Peter Pitchford," Becky exclaimed, looking him over. "Come on, walk with me."

He did as he was asked, and it felt surreal. Was this actually happening? If she asked his age, he would have to lie, no doubt about it. Did she know that he was human? She had to know. He was wondering so many different young worries in those initial moments, this all happening so rapidly that he had to remind himself to breathe.

"Where are we going?" he asked, looking at her profile as they walked side by side. She was even more beautiful this close, he still couldn't believe this.

"We're going to the Mansion, silly!"

"Whoa, whoa," Peter stopped walking. "Seriously, I said I can't go in there. There's no way."

"Oh, come on," she teased him. "Why the heck not?"

"Why the heck not?" he asked back. "Well, for one thing, as you probably have noticed, I'm not a monster. I know what they do to humans in there, so I really don't think I should go in."

Becky leaned in for a mockingly closer look, her proximity sending shivers down his spine.

"I'm not a monster either," she whispered, "and I go in there."

"Wait, what??" Peter asked in confusion, surprised and not quite believing her. "You're a monster, I can tell!"

"Why, because of these horns?" she asked while poking them with her fingers. "You can buy them at the giftshops, you goof! I wanted pink to match my hair, but they didn't have any."

Peter stood dumbfounded. Not only was it a shock that she wasn't a monster, had she really gone into the Brickbat Mansion and survived?

"You're a human like me, and you actually went in there??" he asked, looking to her arms. "Is that what those scars are from?"

Becky instinctively covered them with her hands, her expression changing for a small moment.

LAST FAKE HAPPY WORLD

"...Nope," she answered with a delay. "These aren't from the Mansion. Say, how old are you, anyway?"
From a question that made her uncomfortable to a question that did the same for him. Becky noticed his hesitance and grinned triumphantly, the mood lightening once more.
"Nevermind then, we're not going to the Mansion anymore," she said, grabbing his arm and leading him back the other way.
"Are you sure? You said that you did it, and now that I know you're a human, maybe I could do it too."
"*Peter*," she said in a certain way as she continued dragging him the other direction, "if I can be honest with you, I think there might be something a little more important for you to see."

Within the Brickbat Boulevard, there was another attraction that Peter had never been to. Not only that, but it was a ride that during his previous visit he had no desire to see.
"Are you serious?" he asked with an unsure tone.
"Oh, I'm very serious. I think you need to see what's in there, everybody does."

~ The Tunnel of Love ~

It was a blood water ride, a charcoal hill with a demonic face, each boat only built for two passengers. There was a two-story animatronic of the female Brickbat Bunny mascot beside it, sitting in a suggestive pose with her leg extending up and down. She wore the same black latex suit as the other mascots, rabbit ears and stiletto boots.
"A Tunnel of Love?" Peter asked out of embarrassment and wonder.
"Yeah. It's just a plain old Tunnel of Love. Is that ok with you?"
He had seen versions of this on cartoons and movies, something romantic for a couple to ride on together. But what would this be, something torturous or of no return?

LAST FAKE HAPPY WORLD

"Is it really just that?" he asked, all attention focused away from her and now nervously at the ride.

"Are you seriously scared right now?"

Peter thought about what time it was, thought about his parents and wondered if he should just head back. Was it too soon? But this girl, Becky... He couldn't leave now, especially with her wanting to go on this potentially romantic ride with him. Maybe it was no big deal after all, maybe just a twist on the human version, monsters jumping out or something harmless along those lines.

With his mind adrift, she took his hand and led him through the empty line, to the two-seat boat and they sat in, no safety harnesses or precautions. She seemed excited, her eyes lighting up as she comically shook him, so excited for the thrills yet to come.

The waterway of blood carried their small boat forward, under the kicking mascot's giant leg and through the charcoal face of the hill, into the Tunnel of Love.

Initially, it was wonderful. There were random little scenes of monsters and puppets and things that they both were overjoyed with. Everything was funny for some reason, easing up the tension in his mind. As the early segments continued, Becky leaned against him and then, without even thinking, he somehow mustered the impossible courage to awkwardly slide his arm around her.

She allowed it, and things began changing. It was still a ride, but it felt different, feeling new yet normal. The horrors of 'Black Mass Mountain' were an afterthought for those opening moments. There was no nervousness, there were no monsters beneath human skin or even blood beneath them in the water. There was only the pair of them, riding along together into the unknown.

But something more was coming. The boat wasn't on a track, and it sometimes bounded from the blood's choppy path. They braced themselves as it made them move, sometimes pushing them together, sometimes splitting them apart. The scenes that they saw

LAST FAKE HAPPY WORLD

in the dark were coming to light, at first dim and then too bright, slowly the terrors of the park playing in.

"Try not to get too scared," Becky told him with an only half serious concern on her face. "Love gets a little crazy sometimes."

Peter felt fine, finding himself holding her with both arms now, the boat picking up momentum as if heading somewhere fast. New visions came into sight as the lights flashed fast enough to cause a seizure. He closed his eyes from the repetitious blasting, but it was relentless, consuming his mind until he opened his eyelids again.

What happened next was the most foreign thing yet, a series of events that flew passing by in minutes that somehow felt like years. Confusion and disorientation, the flashing lights, the sights and the rocking of the boat. The animatronic and puppet scenes he saw stirred into the reality of his mind, Peter seeing the darkside sights of this terrible Tunnel of Love.

It was a version of him, a version of Becky, and it was a theater of pain that he watched their performance in. There was the early crush, there was the natural chemical attraction. They kissed and did strange things in this haunting scene of the theme park ride. Peter played along, letting it show him these never-before seen sights and pleasures, his eyes gaping open in the educating light. Becky said nothing, side by side with him still.

Did she see what he was seeing now, too? He thought to ask her, but couldn't think, mesmerized by this adult theater play. The boat propelled past it, Peter turning his head and nearly leaning out of his seat to see every single moment, seeing himself and seeing his new friend in such unconventional activities.

The scenes of superimposed reality continued, but nothing would surpass that opening act. Each additional segment grew worse and more painful. What was this? It was the two of them again, but in a hospital, a waiting room full of odd characters and dim, pulsating lights.

Peter looked at Becky beside him in the boat. She didn't return

LAST FAKE HAPPY WORLD

the gesture.

He returned his eyes to the scene and it had changed, the waiting room was gone and now there was something medical going on. An injection? Becky was in pain, it was something inside of her body. He looked away, but not quickly enough, a cartoon embryo projected onto the wall, liquified and dissolving.

A sickness welled up inside of Peter and he wanted to leave, looking down at the blood water and feeling even worse. He took his arms back from Becky, trying to talk to her but his voice was drowned out, distractions and background voices growing too loud now to even communicate.

The abortion passed, and Peter let it, not looking back to see as he had with the scene that led into it. This ride couldn't go much longer, could it? He looked again to the attraction, and now there were gorgeous women in small pink bikinis, walking around the portrayed version of himself. Becky was there, but in normal clothes, looking completely disconnected. Peter couldn't help but stay focused on the girls, his heart feeling hungry like when he had first set eyes on Becky.

He looked away from the scene and to the real girl sitting beside him, then unable to help but return his sight to the Tunnel of Love.

The women were gone.

Instead, it was a scene now of Becky and himself in an emotional exchange, violent facial expressions leading to a sudden and false calm. There was another medical scene shown, but this time not an abortion. Becky was on a table; massive silicone orbs being stuffed into her sliced open breasts. Why was she doing this?

More flashing lights, and the show continued, the boat going faster through the attraction. He saw Becky in a new scene with her augmented body on display, so perfect now and artificial. They were walking somewhere, shadowed by monsters who stretched and made dangerous advances, drooling and sneaking for a chance to get a better look.

The ride-projected Peter and Becky argued again, about what, the

LAST FAKE HAPPY WORLD

watching Peter didn't know. The monsters constantly loomed in the background, waiting for their moment. Becky cried and ran away in the scene, but that version of Peter didn't follow.

"I don't think I would fight with you like that," Peter tried to say to the real Becky beside him, his words lost and unheard.

The next scene was playing, and he had to look away. A looming monster from the waiting background had seized the opportunity, mounted atop the willing Becky. Peter couldn't block out what he saw, the recaptured look of love on Becky's face that he had seen in the first scene.

What was with this horrible ride? He looked everywhere else to not watch the cheating love display, but even in distraction he could hear the moans of her wild passion. It all felt too real, feeling like she was truthfully betraying him in this screwed up theme park show.

Then the fading, echoing last moan, and all went quiet. The sounds of the simulated reproduction were over. The background music and voice chatter died, the carefree progress of the attraction coming to a lifeless stop. The lights were off.

"Becky? Becky, is it over?"

Peter reached beside himself and felt for her in the emptiness. Nothing. It was only him in the boat now, alone in the dark.

"Becky?" he asked once more, louder this time and still feeling around for anything. "Ok, Becky. This ride kind of sucks, I think maybe we should've went to the Mansion."

He sat there for a while, a long while, with no sense of purpose in his thoughts, his sight refusing to adjust to the black. This ride had been the worst. The electric chair carousel wouldn't have even been able to fry his mind like this. The abortion, the implants, the arguments, the cheating... Why would she cheat on him like that, he wondered? To see it so clearly, and to see that she loved it, something like that was too much to handle.

"It's not real, Peter" he stated out loud to remind himself, trying to be convincing.

LAST FAKE HAPPY WORLD

But it did feel real, so very unforgivingly real, and now it was apparent that she was gone. Was she really with that monster in the scene, abandoning him here alone with nothing?

It was getting hotter and his brain pulled in every direction, his body beginning to sweat. His forearms were covered the most, sweating so profusely that it almost hurt. But still he couldn't stop thinking of the scenes. He couldn't stop thinking of the girl he met, wondering where in the world she had gone, who she was with, or if she even cared. It wasn't supposed to be like this, the Tunnel of Love. Things were supposed to be different.

The music came on and the bright lights returned, not flashing this time, but a blinding, inescapable light.

He put his arms to his eyes, the entire surroundings of the ride illuminated at once. The boat, the blood water, even the walls of the Tunnel of Love interior -

And Peter was bleeding. The heavy sweat on his arms wasn't sweat at all. Deep gashes were slit up and down his forearms, blood dripping from him to the boat's damp floor. How had this happened? But somehow, he knew. Even though he hadn't, apparently in the reality-deception of this attraction, he had mutilated himself. He instantly remembered the scars on Becky's forearms and put it all together. They were the same, they were both hurt at different times in this same bizarre attraction.

And now, for no reason at all, she was back. Becky was here again beside him in the boat, all of this time later.

Peter hugged her hard, sitting side by side like they had before.

"I don't know what's going on," he cried to her, his face buried in her shoulder. "Why did you leave me? Where did you go??"

"It's the Tunnel of Love, silly," she unsuccessfully tried to remind him. "I never left. Even if we stay together, we won't see things the exact same way."

LAST FAKE HAPPY WORLD

"I don't understand any of this," Peter complained, his eyes still fresh with tears. "I was so scared when you left me, I didn't know what to do -"

But before he could continue feeling that emotion, the attraction was alive again. The same as before, the two of them together. But something felt altered and he saw things in a different light. The scene was back to the display of them having intercourse, though this time the real Peter wasn't even interested in watching.

Instead, his eyes stayed on the real Becky, watching her every reaction, wondering what she saw and what these scenes looked like to her. The imagery changed, he could tell, but still he never looked at it again. He didn't want to take his eyes off the real girl before him, worried she would disappear again if he ever looked away.

Scene after scene, sounds of horrible things, a lifetime show of things he didn't want to know. His mind echoed back and forth about her. Did he still like her, or did he ever even like her to begin with? Maybe it was obsession. Did he even really know her, truly understand her inner thoughts? It had to be the effects of this Tunnel of Love ride, but he couldn't look away, it was impossible to trust her.

It was subtle and then obvious, her profile settling in and her skin drying and wrinkling. Peter was mesmerized, watching the once young girl fast forwarding. His eyes had to be playing tricks on him as decades went passing by. The beautiful young girl Becky was now old and withering.

"Peter?" she turned to face him, the real Becky, now aged to the human limit. "Do you... still love me?"

He reached to touch her face, knowing this had to be an illusion.

His hand, it was aged now too? His old forearms showed the healed scars of those self-mutilations from all that time ago.

As he touched Becky's cheek, her skin fell to dust, her lifeless skeletal body falling grimly into his arms.

LAST FAKE HAPPY WORLD

The lights went off, the sound went off, the music died, and Peter sat alone in the darkness one last time. Now in the emptiness of old age, alone at the end of the ride.

That was it? That was all there was to it? After all of these harsh struggles, after all of the pain, it all led to the same oblivion? To be alone, to lose her in the end?

When the Tunnel of Love ride returned from the tunnel, Peter and Becky walked to the exit together. She was the same, but he was changed, something new and indifferent in his eyes.

"So, what did you see?" Becky asked, still a happy tone in her voice. "I can't wait to hear about it, everyone sees it differently, you know? It's creepy how real it seems!"

Peter said nothing, still walking when she stopped.

"...Peter?" she called to him, but he never turned around.

She may have called out his name one more time, or maybe not. Either way, he didn't care. He had just learned what love might be, the darksides of what love could be, and he knew he didn't need it.

"Don't look back," he ordered himself under his breath, purging every happy thought about her from his heart.

With the reminding scars remaining on his arms, he headed back to the Brickbat Mansion to meet up with his family.

He was ready to leave this monster's world and go home to his life again.

To Hell with vacation. To Hell with life in love.

LAST FAKE HAPPY WORLD

From the Author

Greetings from the bitter end. Here we are, later in life and in complete control of a newly refined darkness. It was a strange undertaking for me to write 'Last Fake Happy World.' I've always written long, winding adventures that connected strange creatures and bizarre locations. But this, this was a completely different beast. Seventeen individual stories of complicated days, fast starts and abrupt endings, all with a loose theme injected somewhere within.

In life, what are you supposed to do? While some live their dreams, and some revel in their expected mediocrity, there is a dark balance for others. Finding happiness is always a common goal, but what about when that popular, traditional happiness is eliminated? Not everyone can live in their wish-came-true world, and that was the life spark of Last Fake Happy World. Twisted joy, a single moment of escape, or a fulfilling thought before death. The revenge of a dead deer, young people deciding to live without love, even peace of mind via an annual Halloween massacre.

These unconventional discoveries of something like happiness, however brief or continuous they may be, define the tormented souls within these stories. When we were children, most of us believed what we saw. We believed that if we never gave up, our dreams would come true. We believed that if someone jumped off a building, or shot themselves in the head, they would instantly die.

But where is that magic button? Outside of Hollywood, dreams seldom come true, even with determined passion and hard work. In the real world, maybe that suicide-leap leaves you still alive and paralyzed, or that self-inflected gunshot leaves you brain-dead with half a face. Now what? There's a reason that most mainstream movies have dramatic and happy endings – In your real life, things seldom end so well.

LAST FAKE HAPPY WORLD

And that's where Last Fake Happy World comes in. Mixing my love of fantasy, horror and the supernatural with that real life feeling of a bad ending. At some point, we've all felt it. Some of us a bit more than others, without a doubt. But when that desired happiness is completely out of reach, we can fake it. Fake it until our human brain believes it, fake it until our entire world is engulfed in it. We aren't truly happy, but we find different ways to believe we are, if only for survival.

But sticking strictly to such a theme would be dull, so I tried to capture occult situations. I think of my road trips to old haunted locales, or time spent hiking alone in the deep mountains. I think of those nights meeting strangers at punk clubs, even running away as a kid to try living in the sewer. I've seen so many strange things, I've found myself in so many unusual predicaments. But what if there was more? What if I had vanished, or been eaten? Would I have found that intangible happiness I was searching for in my death, or would it have belonged to the monster that killed me?

Last, but not least, thank you. Thank you to those people who hurt or somehow affected me in a negative capacity. And I don't mean that with a grudge.

There was once a revolving door in my life of people coming in, looking around, then leaving with destruction in their wake. But without their betrayals, without the separation pain or their harsh words, I would have possibly been at a loss to find this continued source of creativity. Sorrow can be an awesome emotion, a feeling that in the end is just as powerful as happiness, if not more. Being alive to really experience it, and to feel its effects on the heart, has brought me an incredible amount of inspiration.

So then, to the souls who have crossed me out, intentionally or not, thank you. Without those gut-wrenching days, there would be far less of this creative drive that has brought me so much joy in life. Across the years, through the 'horror of it all,' I've been thriving despite the disappointing setbacks.

LAST FAKE HAPPY WORLD

I really hope that you've enjoyed this screwed-up journey through the 'Last Fake Happy World' of T.B.O.A. Sad. Hopefully something in this book will worm its way into your head, haunting you for many years to come. In the end, what do we do but live, suffer and die? We look for distractions, we look for happiness. Eventually, it will be your last miserable day in this world. Try to be happy.

~ T.B.O.A. Sad

Please take the time to experience the entire T.B.O.A. Sad world at **tboasad.com** - Experience the handcrafted clothing, toylines and writing of the underground disaster. Contact the author direct at tboasad@gmail.com

LAST FAKE HAPPY WORLD

I.T.H.J. - W.T.B.O. - B.T.O.T. - B.T.O.R.
100035.6x ~ 200083.8x

Find the treasure.